"SHALL WE FIND OUT IF THE SECOND TIME
WE KISS EACH OTHER IS AS WONDERFUL AS
THE FIRST?"

He did not wait for her answer, but his lips were on
hers and Alisa knew at the first touch of them that
this was what she had been longing and yearning for
and thought she would never know again.

The strength of his arms holding her against him and
the wonder of his kiss brought the rapturous feeling
that she had known before, moving through her
breasts, up her throat, and onto her lips.

Then he was carrying her into the sky and they were
one with the stars.

GIFT OF THE GODS

Bantam Books by Barbara Cartland
Ask your bookseller for the books you have missed

125 THE DAWN OF LOVE
126 LUCIFER AND THE ANGEL
127 OLA AND THE SEA WOLF
128 THE PRUDE AND THE PRODIGAL
129 LOVE FOR SALE
130 THE GODDESS AND THE GAIETY GIRL
131 SIGNPOST TO LOVE
132 LOST LAUGHTER
133 FROM HELL TO HEAVEN
134 PRIDE AND THE POOR PRINCESS
135 THE LIONESS AND THE LILY
136 THE KISS OF LIFE
137 AFRAID
138 LOVE IN THE MOON
139 THE WALTZ OF HEARTS
140 DOLLARS FOR THE DUKE
141 DREAMS DO COME TRUE
142 A NIGHT OF GAIETY
143 ENCHANTED
144 WINGED MAGIC
145 A PORTRAIT OF LOVE
146 THE RIVER OF LOVE
147 GIFT OF THE GODS
148 AN INNOCENT IN RUSSIA

Barbara Cartland's Library of Love Series

THE OBSTACLE RACE

About Barbara Cartland

CRUSADER IN PINK

Gift
of the
Gods

Barbara Cartland

BANTAM BOOKS
TORONTO · NEW YORK · LONDON · SYDNEY

GIFT OF THE GODS
A Bantam Book / November 1981

ISBN 0-553-20014-3

Published simultaneously in the United States and Canada

Bantam Books are published by Bantam Books, Inc. Its trademark, consisting of the words "Bantam Books" and the por-
trayal of a rooster, is Registered in U.S. Patent and Trademark
Office and in other countries. Marca Registrada. Bantam
Books, Inc., 666 Fifth Avenue, New York, New York 10103.

Author's Note

The Gunning Sisters, Maria and Elizabeth, arrived in London from Ireland in 1751. They were immediately pronounced "the most beautiful women alive," but they were so poor that for some time they used to share one gown between them.

In 1752, Elizabeth, the younger, married the sixth Duke of Hamilton at half-past-twelve at night at the Mayfair Chapel, with "a ring of the bed-curtain."

She had two sons who both became Dukes of Hamilton, and when her husband died in 1758 she married the Marquis of Lorne, who became the Duke of Argyll.

The elder sister, Maria, married the sixth Earl of Coventry. Because for her beauty she was mobbed in Hyde Park, the King insisted she should have a guard of fourteen soldiers to protect her.

She had five children, but she was only twenty-seven when she died of consumption after her health was upset by using cosmetics containing white lead.

The fascinating little Madame Vestris, the pet of the Regency Bucks and Beaux, was notorious for her amorous interests as well as for her professional accomplishments. She blazed a trail of new attitudes and practises on the stage, and her exquisite legs and her laughter were like a gleam of sunshine.

Chapter One
1821

As Sir Hadrian Wynton was driven away down the unkept drive, which was a complete contrast to the smart carriage in which he was travelling, his daughters gave a sigh of relief.

They had been hustling and bustling from morning until evening during the last few days, getting their father packed up and ready to set off for Scotland.

Sir Hadrian's hobby was geology and he had written erudite but rather dull books on the rocks and stones of Britain.

Therefore, when he received an invitation from an old friend to visit him in Scotland, with the promise that he could not only explore the mountains of Perthshire but also journey to the Shetland Islands, he was as excited as a schoolboy at the idea.

"I have always wanted to research, for one thing, the Pictish forts," he said, "and see what type of stones they used, and I should not be surprised if the Vikings brought with them stones from the other side of the North Sea which up to date have not been discovered."

Penelope, his youngest daughter, made no pretence of listening to her father talk on subjects in which she had no interest.

But Alisa, who loved her father, tried to understand

1

what he was saying, and she knew that, now that her mother was dead, his whole interest was concentrated on what he termed his "work."

She offered to copy out his manuscripts for him in her neat, elegant handwriting before they went to the publishers, and he would even read to her aloud a long chapter when Penelope was either in bed or trying to improve her very scanty wardrobe.

Now as they turned from the front door, having waved their father out of sight, Penelope said:

"I have an idea to tell you about."

Alisa did not answer, and Penelope said insistently:

"Did you hear me, Alisa?"

"I was just wondering if Papa has taken enough warm clothing with him," Alisa answered. "I am sure it is much colder in the North than it is here, and he will go out in all weathers and forget that he is getting older and more prone to coughs and colds."

"Stop fussing over Papa as if you were a hen with only one chick!" Penelope exclaimed. "And come into the Sitting-Room. I really have something very serious to talk to you about."

She had by now alerted her sister, and Alisa looked at her with startled eyes as she followed Penelope from the Hall into the untidy but comfortable Sitting-Room which in her mother's time had been called the Morning-Room.

Now it was where Alisa and Penelope pursued their special hobbies, and in consequence there was a half-finished gown thrown over one chair with a work-basket open beside it, and on the small easel by the window a picture which Alisa was painting of some primroses in a china vase.

There were a great number of books in the room, too many to find places in the large Chippendale bookcase which was already full.

Many therefore stood rather untidily in one corner, and there were also little piles of two or three on most of the tables.

Alisa was the "reader" and Penelope the "do-er," and they were very different in character, although in looks they were not unalike.

At the same time, there was a difference.

Both were lovely, almost outstandingly beautiful, but Penelope was undoubtedly the more spectacular.

It was impossible to think that any girl could present such an ideal of prettiness.

Her hair was the gold of ripening corn, her eyes as blue as a summer sky, her complexion the pink-and-white that was to be found more often in poems than in actual fact.

People when they saw Penelope thought she could not be real, then when they looked at Alisa and looked again, they realised that she was as lovely as her sister, and yet it was not so obvious.

It was their father who, in one of his more perceptive moods, had christened them "the Rose and the Violet," and it actually was an extremely apt title, which he then forgot because he seldom had time to think about his daughters.

In fact it was only two days before he left for Scotland that he said to Alisa:

"Oh, by the way, Alisa, I have written to your Aunt Harriet and asked her to have you to stay."

"Aunt Harriet? Oh, no, Papa!" Alisa exclaimed involuntarily.

"What do you mean by that?" her father enquired.

There was a pause, then Alisa said:

"I suppose we . . . could not . . . stay here? We would be quite . . . safe, as you well know, with the Brigstocks to look after us."

"The Brigstocks are servants," her father replied,

"and although it has been all right for me to leave you with them for a night or two, it is quite a different thing to be away for two or perhaps three months."

Alisa did not reply.

She was racking her brains to think of somebody they could invite to stay with them instead of having to leave the country she loved and stay with their aunt in London.

They had been to her twice before for short visits and had found it incredibly boring, and she knew that Penelope found the atmosphere of the house in Islington unbearable.

Sir Hadrian's elder sister had married, long before he had, an Army Officer.

General Ledbury had had a long career in the Army, being what her father called scornfully "an armchair soldier," which meant that he spent his time at the War Office and never saw active service.

On his retirement he was awarded the K.C.B., then died, leaving his wife with little money and no children.

This was perhaps the reason why Lady Ledbury took up good works and spent her time working to raise money either for Missionaries, crippled soldiers or orphaned children.

Whenever her nieces stayed with her they were forced to spend their time either making ugly garments for natives in far-off places who found it much more convenient to go naked, or copying out tracts which the Society concerned found too expensive to have printed.

The idea of spending two to three months on such activities was appalling, but as her father was adamant that they could not stay at home, Alisa, who disliked arguing with him, accepted that there was nothing they could do but hope that he would return as quickly as possible.

Now, looking around their Sitting-Room, she thought

despondently that her aunt would never allow her to waste time in painting, and if Penelope wished to sew for herself she would have to do it secretly after she was supposed to be in bed.

Penelope, however; was smiling and there was a look of excitement in her large eyes that made Alisa ask in surprise:

"What is it? What has happened?"

"I have a wonderful idea!" Penelope replied. "And it is all because of something Eloise said to me yesterday."

Eloise Kingston was the daughter of the local Squire, with whom the girls had shared lessons until she had been sent away a year ago to a smart Seminary for Young Ladies.

She had come home a week ago and Penelope had seen her, while Alisa had been too busy packing for her father to be able to visit The Hall.

"I am longing to see Eloise," Alisa said now. "Is she excited at having left School?"

"She is going to be presented at a 'Drawing-Room' at the end of this month," Penelope replied.

For a moment the light had gone from her eyes and there was a bitter note in her voice.

Only Alisa knew how much Penelope resented that Eloise could have the chance to go to Court, to attend Balls, Receptions, and Assemblies in London, while she had to stay at home.

"It is unfair!" she had said over and over again. "Why should Papa not do something for us?"

"The answer is that he cannot afford to," Alisa had replied. "As you well know, Penelope, it is a struggle for us to live here as it is."

"Then why cannot Papa write a book which would make money, instead of producing those dreary old tomes that nobody wants to read?"

Alisa had smiled.

"I do not think it has ever struck Papa that he should

be a wage-earner. I am sure he would think it beneath his dignity."

"We cannot eat the family tree, nor does the fact that Papa is the seventh Baronet buy me a new gown!" Penelope snapped crossly.

Things might not have been so boring if Eloise, who was extremely fond of both of them, had not spent every moment, when she was at home, telling them of the people she had met and the entertainments planned for her in the coming Season.

At Christmas the Squire and his wife had settled down to consider how they could launch their only daughter into the *Beau Monde*.

The Squire was well known in Hertfordshire and was a large landowner, but London was different, and the famous hostesses would not be likely to include Eloise among their guests unless her parents contrived to be socially recognised.

They had been partly successful, for Eloise, according to Penelope, had already received invitations to various Balls that were to take place next month, and the reason she had delayed coming home after her time at the Seminary was finished was that her mother was buying her new gowns.

"I have never seen anything so beautiful!" Penelope had explained in awestruck tones when she had described them to her sister. "The latest fashions are quite, quite different from anything we have been wearing."

Her voice was lyrical as she went on:

"Skirts are fuller round the hem and very elaborately trimmed with lace, flowers, and embroidery, and although the waist is still high, the sleeves are full, while the bonnets are so beautiful that they are indescribable."

Alisa could not help thinking that it was a mistake for Eloise to make Penelope so jealous of her possessions, but she knew it would be wrong to say so.

She thought it would be a good thing when the Squire, his wife, and their daughter left the country for London.

Now thinking that she would have to listen to another rapturous description of Eloise's clothes, Alisa sat down on the sofa and waited for Penelope to tell her what was on her mind.

"Eloise was talking about two girls called the Gunning Sisters," Penelope said. "When they were eighteen they arrived in London from Ireland, and although they were both exceedingly beautiful they had no money."

Alisa smiled.

"I know the story," she said. "I read it ages ago and I told you about it."

"I suppose I was not listening," Penelope replied. "The younger sister married two Dukes, Hamilton and Argyll, and the elder married the Earl of Coventry."

"And she died when she was very young," Alisa added, "from using a face-cream to improve her skin that contained white lead."

"There is no need for you to do that."

Alisa's eyes widened.

"Why should I want to?" she enquired.

"Because we are going to be the Gunning Sisters!" Penelope answered. "I have thought it all out, and I know, however modest you may try to be, that we are just as beautiful as they were."

Alisa laughed.

"I am quite prepared to agree with you, dearest, but it is very improbable that two Dukes will drop down the chimney or an Earl come through the window!"

"Have you forgotten," Penelope asked, "that we are going to London?"

"To be honest, I am depressed at the thought," Alisa answered. "The only men Aunt Harriet entertains, as you are well aware, are Parsons and Missionaries."

"Nevertheless, Aunt Harriet lives in London."

"But how does that help us?"

Penelope was silent for a moment, then she said:

"I am absolutely certain that if you and I had a chance to appear at any of the parties to which Eloise has been invited; we should have the same sensational success as the Gunning Sisters."

Alisa laughed again.

"I think that is unlikely. And we would look like beggars at a Ball, dressed we are now, with everybody else wearing the new gowns which you have described so eloquently."

"The Gunning Sisters had one gown," Penelope said, "so when one went out, the other one had to stay in bed. We are going to have two gowns, one for you and one for me!"

She saw that her sister looked surprised and went on:

"Mrs. Kingston said something to me the other day which made me realise that, unlike the Gunning Sisters, being together is important."

Alisa looked puzzled and Penelope continued:

"She was talking about the vases on the mantelpiece—you know, the Sèvres china ones in the Drawing-Room. As I have known them for years, I suddenly realised there was only one there instead of two.

"'What has happened to the other Sèvres vase, Ma'am?' I enquired.

"Mrs. Kingston sighed and answered:

"'One of the housemaids smashed it last week. I was very angry with the tiresome woman, because you know as well as I do that Sèvres china is valuable, but a pair are worth far more than just one by itself.'"

"I have an idea what you are trying to say," Alisa said. "But I am still wondering how, even if we were invited to a Ball, we could afford one gown, let alone two."

She got up from the sofa on which she had been sitting and said:

"Oh, dearest, I know you mind so much not being able to come out and do the things that Eloise can. But as it says in the Bible, it is no good 'kicking against the pricks'! We just have to accept things as they are and make the best of them."

As she spoke, she put her arm round her younger sister and kissed her cheek.

To her surprise, instead of responding as Penelope usually did to any expression of affection, she merely moved away, saying in a hard, determined little voice:

"I have every intention of 'kicking against the pricks,' as you put it, and what is more, I will not lie down and let fate, or rather poverty, trample all over me!"

She looked so lovely, even when she was irritated, that Alisa could understand her frustrations.

She knew that Penelope was rather like her father, determined to the point of obstinacy when he wished to do something, while she was like her mother, compliant, gentle, and ready to accept the inevitable.

"We have to have money for new gowns," Penelope said, speaking as much to herself as to Alisa.

Then suddenly she gave a scream that seemed to echo round the room.

"I have thought of what we can do!"

"To obtain money?" Alisa asked.

"Yes," Penelope replied. "I remember now something Mrs. Kingston said at tea yesterday when she was gossipping about people who have already asked Eloise to their parties. One woman was a Lady Harrison, whom Mrs. Kingston had known when she was at School.

"'She is very smart these days,' Mrs. Kingston said, 'because her husband is permanently in attendance on the new King.'

"She drivelled on for some time," Penelope went on, "you know how she does. Then she said something that I have just remembered."

"What is it?" Alisa asked.

"She said: 'Of course Lady Harrison tries to keep young by using salves and lotions, dozens of them, which she tells me she buys in Bond Street from Mrs. Lulworth, and do you know that even the smallest pot of cream to restore the roses in her cheeks costs as much as a pound?' "

Penelope stopped speaking and looked at Alisa.

Then, as if she knew she was expected to say something, Alisa remarked:

"It seems a terrible lot of money. I wonder if it does any good."

"If it does not, then that is exactly what we want."

"What are you saying?" Alisa enquired. "I do not understand."

"Oh, dearest, you are being very thick-headed!" Penelope exclaimed. "Suppose you and I sell the creams that Mama used and which we now have to make for ourselves and which do improve the skin? Remember we gave some to that ugly Cosnet child two months ago, who had sores and blemishes on her cheeks, and they healed in four days?"

"Are you saying . . . are you suggesting . . . ?" Alisa started.

"I am telling you," Penelope interrupted, "that that is how we are going to make enough money to buy four gowns—one each for the morning and one each for the evening!"

"You are crazy!" Alisa exclaimed. "Nobody would pay us a pound for our creams, good though they are. All Mrs. Cosnet gave us for our trouble was a bunch of daffodils from her garden!"

"I was not thinking of selling them to Mrs. Cosnet or people like her, stupid!" Penelope said impatiently. "We are going to make the creams and sell them to women like Lady Harrison, who would pay anything to try to look as beautiful as they did when they were young."

"It is an impossible idea! Besides, what would Papa say?"

"Papa will not know for at least two months, by which time the Season will be over. And you know as well as I do that as it is Coronation Year, it is going to be the most exciting, glamorous summer that has ever happened!"

Alisa knew that was true.

The Regent, who had waited so long to become King and was now at fifty-eight an old man, was to be crowned in July.

If the newspapers were to be believed, already London was filling up not only with the English nobility coming in from the country for the festivities, but with foreigners from all over Europe.

"If we make quite a number of Mama's creams," Penelope was saying, "and think up wonderful names for them so that they will sound attractive, it will make people eager to buy them."

"Are you really suggesting," Alisa asked, "that we should take them to London to Mrs. Lulworth and sell them as if we were pedlars?"

"I am prepared to sell anything so that we can buy gowns, and what does it matter what Mrs. Lulworth thinks? She has never seen us before, and unless we have money she is never likely to see us again!"

This was unanswerable, and as Penelope went on pleading and persuading, Alisa found herself weakening.

There was no doubt that her mother's herbal products, which she had made from the flowers, herbs, and plants in their garden, had been a success locally.

People with sores and abrasions of every sort had begged her help, and they also found that the tisanes she made could soothe and reduce a fever and remove a cough far more effectively than anything the Doctors could prescribe.

Her two daughters had always helped her in the Still-Room, but not until this moment had Alisa thought that anything they might make could be saleable.

"If we sell twenty pots at ten shillings each," Penelope said in a practical way, "which Mrs. Lulworth could then sell for a pound, that would be enough for one gown."

"We are not even certain that this Mrs. Lulworth will take them."

"At least we can try, and I am not going to London dressed as I am now. I refuse! I shall stay here all by myself until Papa returns."

"What does it matter what we look like in Islington?" Alisa asked almost beneath her breath.

This was undoubtedly true, and it made Penelope more determined than ever that they would have to get some money by hook or by crook so that, like the Gunning Sisters, they could dazzle Society.

"In any case," Alisa went on, "even if we do make a little money, that will not get us invitations to the Balls or even to the Receptions of anybody of importance."

"I have thought of that too," Penelope said.

Alisa waited apprehensively.

The ideas that Penelope had already expressed were frightening her.

"Do you remember how Mama used to talk about a friend of hers she used to stay with when she was young, a woman by the name of Elizabeth Denison?" Penelope asked.

She did not wait for Alisa to answer, but went on:

"I realised only the other day that she is now the Marchioness of Conyngham, whose name often appears in the newspapers."

"The Marchioness did not pay much attention to Mama after she married," Alisa commented.

"How could she, when Mama was buried down here with Papa? And Elizabeth Denison, who was older than Mama, was very rich."

Alisa was silent, knowing that her mother had been far too proud ever to ask favours of anybody.

If her friend had drifted away into a higher social circle, she would never have tried to cling to her for old times' sake.

"What we are going to do," Penelope went on, "and I thought this out last night, is to write to the Marchioness of Conyngham when we reach London, telling her that Mama is dead and that we have a little memento of her when she was a girl which we are sure she would like to have."

"How could we do such a thing?" Alisa asked indignantly.

"It is something I have every intention of doing," Penelope declared. "Oh, Alisa, do stop being stuffy and realise that the one thing Mama would have hated would be for us to be incarcerated here as if we were shut up in a tomb, seeing nobody, going nowhere, and just wasting our beauty!"

Penelope spoke so passionately that Alisa was silent.

She knew it was true that her mother, who had been completely happy living in the country because she loved her husband, would have wanted them to enjoy the life she had known when she was a girl.

Her parents had been important in Hampshire, where her father had a large Estate, and they had always gone to London for the Season.

When their only daughter grew up, she had been presented at Court to the King and Queen and had a Season whose gaieties had been described over and over again to her daughters when they were old enough to understand.

However, three months after their mother had made her dèbut, she became engaged to Sir Hadrian, and they had been married in the autumn, to live, as Alisa had often said with a smile, "happily ever after."

Unfortunately, during the long-drawn-out war, Sir Hadrian's fortune had dwindled year by year, and when his wife's father died he left everything he possessed to his son.

Then, soon after he came into his inheritance, their uncle had been killed fighting with Wellington's Armies and the Estate went not to his sister but to a distant cousin of the same name.

Alisa knew that Penelope was speaking the truth when she said it would have upset her mother if she had known how dull it was for them these days, and how seldom her father entertained, with the consequence that they were rarely invited to other houses in the neighbourhood.

Another reason for this was obvious.

"We are too pretty and attractive, that is what is wrong with us," Penelope had said last week. "I heard from Mrs. Kingston that the Hartmans are giving a small dance next month but there will be no invitation for us."

"I think it is rather unkind of them not to invite us." Alisa agreed.

"Unkind? They are just taking precautions against our taking away any young man who might be interested in that plain, tongue-tied Alice, or that spotty-faced Charlotte!"

"You should not say such unkind things!"

"It is true! You know it is true!" Penelope insisted. "What man, if he could dance with you or me, would want to trundle round a dance-floor with them? They are both as heavy as a sack of coals!"

Alisa laughed as if she could not help it.

Although she hesitated to agree with Penelope, she had seen the expression on Mrs. Hartman's face the last time they had been there, when Colonel Hartman had told them how pretty they were and made them sit one on either side of him at luncheon.

Because she felt agitated, Alisa went to the window. The lawn was unkept, but there was a carpet of golden daffodils under the trees and the almond-blossoms were pink and white against the sky.

"It is so lovely here!" she said. "We ought to be content."

"Well, I am not!" Penelope replied positively. "So please, please, Alisa, help me! I have nobody else to turn to but you."

It was a cry that went straight to Alisa's soft heart and it was impossible for her to refuse.

Ten minutes later, she agreed to what she thought was the wildest, most ridiculous scheme Penelope had ever suggested.

"We will try to sell Mama's face-creams," she agreed, "but I will take them to London alone."

"You will never sell them as well as I could," Penelope said.

"Yes, I will, if they are saleable," Alisa answered, "and you have convinced me that they are. What I think would be a mistake, dearest, would be for you to be seen selling in the shops in Bond Street where, if we are successful, we shall have to buy our clothes."

She saw that she had made a point, and as Penelope was silent she went on:

"As you well know, I am not half as striking as you are, and I think the wise thing to do would be to take just two or three pots to Mrs. Lulworth and ask if she thinks they are saleable. If she says 'yes,' then we can go ahead and make her many more."

She hesitated a moment, then she said:

"Perhaps we could then swear her to secrecy, and instead of giving us money she might let us have the gowns now and pay for them month by month as the demand for the creams increases."

Penelope clapped her hands together, then flung her arms round Alisa.

"Dearest, you are so clever!" she said. "I knew you would be sensible about my idea, once I had convinced you that it was necessary."

"Of course it is necessary," Alisa agreed. "It is just that I am not certain that this method will obtain the gowns we need."

"Right or wrong, there is no alternative," Penelope said. "Even if we wanted to sell a picture or a mirror off the walls, we would not know how to go about it."

"We could not do that!" Alisa exclaimed in horror. "That would be stealing from Papa!"

Penelope smiled.

"I was sure that was what you would feel. But if you ask me, I do not believe that Papa, if he had his nose in one of his books, would notice if we took down half the house."

This was indisputable, but Alisa was not prepared to go further in that direction.

"We will sell only what is ours," she said firmly, "and the first thing is to prove that face-creams are saleable."

*   *   *

Two days later, Penelope saw Alisa off on the Stage-Coach which stopped at the crossroads in the centre of the village.

They had been hurrying about since dawn, for it was important that Alisa should have time to sell the creams and return on the Coach which passed through the village at six o'clock in the evening.

"If you miss it," Penelope said warningly, "you will have to stay the night with Aunt Harriet, and she will think it very strange that you should go to London by yourself."

"I shall have masses of time," Alisa answered. "In fact I shall find it rather frightening to be alone in

London unless I go to the waiting-room at the Two-Headed Swam and just sit there until the Stage-Coach arrives."

"That would be a sensible thing to do," Penelope approved, "but I think really I should come with you."

"No, no," Alisa answered.

She knew only too well that whatever Penelope wore she would attract attention. Although she knew it was wrong for either of them to go to London alone, it was impossible to ask Mrs. Brigstock to accompany her, because she was too old.

Emily, the girl who came in to scrub the floors, was too uncouth, and what was more she was certain to talk of what happened to everybody in the village.

"I must go alone," she told herself, "and as I shall be dressed quietly, nobody will notice me."

Because she was not only nervous but more than a little frightened, she picked out a very plain dark-blue gown and a plain straight cape that had belonged to her mother to wear over it.

Although her bonnet was cheap, it had been trimmed skilfully with flowers. These Alisa removed, leaving only the ribbons round the crown and those under her chin.

"You look like a Puritan," Penelope said as they walked up to the crossroads.

"Perhaps I should hold one of Aunt Harriet's tracts in my hand," Alisa said with a note of laughter in her voice. "Then I would be quite certain that nobody will pay any attention to me!"

"If I have to sit night after night in that gloomy house in Islington," Penelope argued, "listening to Aunt Harriet talking about 'the poor blacks in Africa,' I shall throw myself into the Serpentine!"

"Then I hope some dashing young gentleman would dive in and save you!" Alisa laughed.

"I expect I would simply be fished out by some old

man with a boat-hook!" Penelope retorted. "So save me
by selling those creams."

They had both taken the greatest trouble in mixing
the creams exactly as their mother had done. One
contained fresh cucumbers from the garden, herbs, and
a number of other ingredients of which fortunately they
had quite a large supply.

Before Sir Hadrian had left, he had given Alisa ten
pounds.

"If you take the Coach to London," he had said, "it
will leave you enough to tip your aunt's servants and to
pay for anything that is absolutely necessary. I have
given the Brigstocks their wages for two months, and I
cannot afford any more."

"No, I understand, Papa," Alisa had said.

She knew that although he was being driven to
Scotland with his friend, he would still have quite a
number of expenses when he was there.

Leaving so early in the morning, the Stage-Coach
contained inside only two farmers' wives journeying as
far as the next market-town.

The men, who were mostly farmers, preferred to sit
on the box, but Alisa noticed that young or old they all
turned to stare at Penelope as she kissed her good-bye.

'It is a good thing she is not coming with me,' she
thought.

As soon as the Stage-Coach started off, she waved to
her sister, then sat comfortably in a corner-seat and
soon got into conversation with the farmers' wives.

All they wanted to talk about was the coming Coronation and the village festivities which would take place to
celebrate the occasion.

"Well, all Oi can say is 'e's had a good time, one way
or another," one woman said, "an' at least 'e's given us
all somethin' to talk about."

"Not the sort of talk Oi cares for," another answered.
"Debts an' women are a bad example, that's wot Oi says

to me lads. Ye pays yer way as ye goes, Oi tells 'em, or Oi'll have somethin' to say about it."

'That is what we will have to do,' Alisa thought to herself, and she felt despondently that the sale of a few pots of cream could not possibly pay for all the things that Penelope wanted.

It was still early in the morning when she reached London, and because she had plenty of time she started to walk from Islington to Bond Street.

It was no hardship, because Alisa was used to walking long distances, since although she preferred to ride they had been too hard up these last years to afford more than two horses. This meant that she and Penelope had been forced to take it in turns to go out hunting with their father or to ride wherever they wished to go.

"It has been rather like sharing a gown!" she told herself now.

She found herself thinking of the huge success which the Gunning Sisters had achieved entirely because they were beautiful.

She was not sure that she herself was beautiful, although she was not so foolish as not to acknowledge that she was pretty. But she thought nobody could be lovelier than Penelope.

She now decided that she had been remiss in not speaking to her father, before he left for Scotland, about Penelope having a chance to meet the type of young man she should eventually marry.

"After all, it was my duty to do that," Alisa chided herself. "I am the elder."

She was actually eighteen months older than Penelope, who had just celebrated her seventeenth birthday.

Alisa knew that things would not have come to such a pass if her father had not gone away or Eloise Kingston had not made Penelope envious by talking so much about her own prospects.

"What chance have we," Alisa asked herself, "of meeting, as Mama did, somebody like Papa?"

She knew that her father must have looked very handsome in his uniform.

He had been in the Grenadier Guards, and in his red coat, white breeches, and bear-skin, she could understand that her mother had found him irresistible.

'And Papa loved her,' Alisa thought.

It was the sort of marriage she herself would like to make, for while Penelope wanted to have an important social position and wear a tiara and glittering jewels at Carlton House and the Royal Pavilion at Brighton, she would be quite content to be anywhere as long as she was with the man whom she loved and who loved her.

'I suppose I am not ambitious,' she thought with a sigh.

Then she told herself, although it was something she would not say to anybody, not even to Penelope, that love if one found it would be so wonderful, so glorious, that there was nothing else with which to compare it.

Walking through the streets, she found herself fascinated by the pedlars who were already crying their wares.

There were men carrying pails of milk fresh from the cow, women with baskets of primroses and daffodils, and others with country produce like butter and new-laid eggs.

Having been in London before, she knew the way to Bond Street, and when she finally reached that most fascinating shopping street in the city, she could not help staring in the shop-windows and finding them extremely inviting after having been in the country for so long.

She saw at once, as Penelope had said, that the clothes they were wearing were out-of-fashion. The new bonnets had crowns that were raised in front and

were covered with ostrich-feathers or a profusion of silk
flowers.

Alisa stood for some time outside one window, trying
to see if it was possible to transform their outdated
head-gear into something that at least reflected, if
indecisively, the vogue.

She decided it was just possible that she might be
able to do something with what they already possessed,
when a man stopped beside her and she knew in a
sudden panic that he was about to speak to her.

Quickly she walked away, just as his lips began to
move, and she told herself that it was entirely her own
fault for loitering.

With her heart beating rather quickly, she hurried
down the street to where she thought Mrs. Lulworth's
shop would be situated.

It was a large Emporium that sold quite a number of
things besides gowns, and already there were a few
customers fingering some very attractive and doubtless
extremely expensive silks at a counter near the door.

Not daring to stop and stare into the window, she
had, however, noted at a quick glance that elegantly
displayed on a silk cushion were several glass bottles
and what looked like a pot of face-cream.

"Can I assist you, Madam?"

It was a supercilious shop-assistant who spoke, and
for a moment Alisa thought it was impossible to tell him
the reason why she was there. Then she forced herself
to say:

"Could I . . . please see . . . Mrs. Lulworth?"

She thought that the shop-assistant looked her up
and down and took in her shabby appearance before he
replied:

"Could I enquire as to your requirements?"

Alisa lifted her chin a little.

"It is a private matter, and I would ask you to take

me to her immediately!" she replied, speaking in what she hoped was a commanding and dignified manner.

As it happened, her voice was so musical, and when he looked under her bonnet her face was so pretty, that the shop-assistant, who was more perceptive than he looked, decided to do what was asked without further argument.

"If you will come this way, Madam," he said, and swept ahead to where farther in the shop were a number of gowns and bonnets on display.

Standing in front of a cowed-looking shop-girl was a large woman dressed in black.

She was obviously complaining about something very volubly, until Alisa appeared, and when the assistant said: "Someone to see you, Madam," she turned, and there was a smile on her lips that was obviously put on for effect.

The assistant she had been berating hurried away as if relieved at being released, and the shop-assistant also disappeared, as if he was sure he had made a mistake.

"What can I do for you—*Madame?*"

There was a little pause before the last word, which made it quite clear that Mrs. Lulworth thought she was not entitled to it.

For a moment Alisa felt as if her courage failed her. It was impossible for her to speak, and it would have been far easier to leave without attempting to sell anything.

Then she thought of Penelope's disappointment, and she steeled herself.

She also remembered what Penelope had told her to say because she was certain it would make an impression.

"I understand . . . Mrs. Lulworth . . ." Alisa began, with only a slight tremor in her voice, "that Lady Harrison purchases from you some excellent face-creams."

"That is true, and Her Ladyship has been very satisfied."

"I have here some . . . face-creams that are far . . . superior to anything Lady Harrison has . . . tried so far. I have brought them hoping you might be . . . interested in . . . selling them."

There was a little pause before Mrs. Lulworth asked:

"You are saying that you make face-creams?"

"Yes."

"And they are good?"

"Very, very good! Everybody near where we live in the country begs us to help them when they have any sort of trouble with their skin. And after they have used these creams, the trouble vanishes almost at once!"

Mrs. Lulworth looked sceptical, but while she had been talking Alisa had opened the silk bag she carried, which contained three pots of cream.

"Will you please look at the creams, Mrs. Lulworth?" she begged. "The one with the green ribbon round it is called *The Freshness of Spring*."

Mrs. Lulworth made a sound that was untranslatable but might have indicated either approval or disgust.

Alisa drew out the other pots. One, called *Golden Wonder*, contained cowslips, and the other, which had been made from the first carrots that had appeared in the garden, was *Red Sunrise*.

Mrs. Lulworth tested each one by rubbing it into the skin of her left hand. It was an old hand with the veins showing prominently, the skin darkened by what the country-folk called "sun-spots" but which Alisa knew always appeared with old age.

Then sharply, so that Alisa almost jumped, Mrs. Lulworth asked:

"Do you use these creams yourself?"

"Yes, always," Alisa answered.

"You swear that is true?" Mrs. Lulworth persisted, staring at Alisa's smooth and flawless cheeks, which had just a touch of color in them because she was agitated.

"I swear it!" Alisa answered. "And my sister also uses them."

She knew as she spoke that it was quite unnecessary to involve Penelope, but Mrs. Lulworth appeared to be thinking.

Then she asked:

"How much do you expect me to pay you for this cream?"

Alisa hesitated.

"I . . . understand that Lady Harrison pays over . . . a pound for a pot of your cream . . . and I thought . . . if I sell mine to you at ten shillings a pot . . . that would be fair."

Mrs. Lulworth gave a scornful laugh.

"And how, young woman," she asked, "do you think I should pay the rent and the services of my staff and stock my shelves and cupboards without getting into debt, if I took so small a profit?"

Alisa felt her spirits sink.

She might have guessed, she thought, that Penelope had been too optimistic in anticipating that they would be paid so much.

Then, perhaps because she looked so crestfallen and at the same time so young, while her skin in the morning light coming through the window had a translucence about it, like a pearl that had just been raised from its oyster-bed, Mrs. Lulworth said:

"I tell you what I'll do—I will send you to a very good customer of mine who has, as it happens, just sent a message asking for something new for her skin. When you arrived, I was wondering what I should reply."

Alisa's eyes were bright again with hope as Mrs. Lulworth went on:

"I am going to tell you now to go to this important customer and show her these creams. If she takes them, and if she likes them, then I'll buy from you quite a number of pots, because half of London will follow her example. Is that clear?"

"Oh, thank you . . . thank you!" Alisa cried. "I am sure she will like them."

Mrs. Lulworth shrugged her shoulders.

"She may, or she may not. She's unpredictable, and if she's in one of her tantrums she'll be more likely to throw the pots at you than to buy them!"

Alisa looked apprehensive, and involuntarily her fingers tightened on the bag she was still holding in her hand.

"Are you willing to test your luck?" Mrs. Lulworth asked. "If you can't sell your wares where they are most needed, then they are of no use to me."

Her shrewd eyes were still looking at Alisa's flawless skin, as if she could not believe it was real and not some trick of the light.

Then she said:

"Well, be off with you. I'll be interested to hear *Madame* Vestris's opinion of what you have to sell, so come back here after you have seen her."

"*Madame* . . . Vestris?" Alisa questioned, thinking she could not have heard the name aright.

"*Madame* Vestris at the King's Theatre. She tells me they're having a rehearsal there this morning, and so whether she'll be in a good temper or a bad one depends on how it is going. You'll just have to take your chance."

"*Madame* Vestris—the King's Theatre!" Alisa repeated, as if she was afraid she might forget.

"What are you waiting for?" Mrs. Lulworth asked. "Go there and don't bother to come back unless the 'Prima Donna,' as she fancies herself, has made a purchase."

"Thank you," Alisa said.

She put the pots back into her silk bag, then walked through the shop and out into Bond Street.

Chapter Two

It was not a very long way from Bond Street to the King's Theatre in the Haymarket, but Alisa hurried along, frightened that if she was late, *Madame* Vestris would have left and she would not be able to see her.

As she went, she was trying to remember all she knew about the actress, which was actually a good deal.

Penelope was extremely interested in anything that concerned the Theatre, simply because they very seldom were able to go to one.

When their mother was alive she had insisted that their father take them to the Opera, which she thought was good for their education, and they had several times been to a Shakespearean Play.

It was Penelope who talked about *Madame* Vestris, who had, according to the newspapers, captivated the town when she first appeared in London five weeks after the Battle of Waterloo.

Alisa remembered Penelope telling her that Lucy Vestris, who was the daughter of an artist, was then married to an Italian who was also an actor.

The newspapers always described her as being vivacious, extremely pretty, and having, although it sounded rather improper, the most exquisite legs on the stage.

For some years her success appeared to have been due to her dancing, then last year the newspapers had made the sensational announcement that *Madame* Vestris was to appear as a man in a new Operetta called *Giovanni in London*.

This was something which for an actress was sensational, and it was said that *Madame* Vestris accepted the part with much reluctance.

Thinking back over what she had read herself and what Penelope had read aloud, Alisa remembered that *Madame* had had an overwhelmingly favourable reception and the Theatre had been packed night after night to see her famous legs.

"I think it is very brave of her," Penelope had said.

"But ... surely it is somewhat ... immodest?" Alisa had replied hesitatingly.

They had argued about it until Alisa had for once got the better of her sister by producing a notice which criticised *Madame* Vestris by saying:

> *It is the part which no female should assume until she has discarded every delicate scruple by which her mind or her person can be distinguished.*

"Well, I refuse to agree to that until I have seen her for myself," Penelope had answered, "and I think it would be rather fun to dress as a man."

"Really, Penelope, what will you think of next?" Alisa had cried.

At the same time, she could not help feeling it would be very exciting to see *Giovanni in London*, but when Penelope suggested it to her father, he said it was certainly not the type of entertainment for young girls.

'What a pity Penelope is not with me now,' Alisa thought as she walked towards the King's Theatre.

Then she reflected that it would have been a great mistake, because undoubtedly Penelope would have got a new idea: that they should both go on the stage to make money.

It made her laugh to think of anything so ridiculous!

When she reached the King's Theatre she was aware that an actress would go in through the stage-door, and she was relieved when she saw that it was open and knew that therefore the rehearsal could not be over.

However, there was always the chance that *Madame* Vestris might have left early.

Apprehensively she hurried to where an elderly man with white hair sat just inside the door in what looked like a glass box.

"I would like, please, to see *Madame* Vestris."

"That's not very likely, Miss, unless ye've got an appointment!"

"I have brought something *Madame* requires from Mrs. Lulworth," Alisa answered.

"The shop in Bond Street?"

"That is right."

"Then I expect her'll see ye."

He came out of his box and started to hurry along a dark passage with a stone floor which made Alisa aware that the back of the stage was certainly not as attractive as the Auditorium.

She followed the old man for quite some way until she saw several doors with names painted on them, from behind which came the sounds of voices and laughter.

It made her more nervous than she was already. The old man stopped and said:

"Wait here!"

Holding tightly to the bag that contained the pots of cream, Alisa sent up a little prayer that she might be successful in selling them.

She was quite certain that if *Madame* Vestris tried any of the creams, she would be delighted with them.

Nobody had ever failed to find them healing, and people returned year after year for more of her mother's herbs in whatever form they appeared.

The old man had knocked on the door ahead, which she saw was marked in large white letters: MADAME VESTRIS.

As he did so, a door on the other side of the corridor opened and three women dressed in gowns which they obviously wore on the stage came out laughing and talking to one another.

Close up, their gowns looked tawdry and to Alisa's eyes were cut so low as to be indecent.

She moved to one side to let them pass, and there was a strong fragrance of a musty perfume that was overpowering and lingered on the air even after the women were out of sight.

Then she could hear the voice of the old man speaking to somebody, and again she was afraid that *Madame* Vestris might be, as Mrs. Lulworth had warned her, in one of her tantrums.

There had been some rather unkind references in the newspapers to her temperament, and Penelope had said, although how she knew was a mystery, that all great actresses and Prima Donnas made scenes and flounced about the stage, upsetting the other actors just to show their superiority.

After what seemed a long time, although it was only a few minutes, Alisa saw the old man returning.

"'Er'll see ye," he said laconically, jerking his thumb at the door he had left open behind him, before he limped away down the corridor.

Alisa moved to the open door, wishing that she had not come, but at the same time determined that for Penelope's sake she would do everything in her power to make *Madame* Vestris buy their creams.

The dressing-room was exactly as she had expected it to be, except that it was larger and there were more flowers. But for the moment it was impossible to look at anything except a small figure standing in the centre of it—a woman wearing breeches!

Everything Alisa had been going to say went out of her head and she could only stare at *Madame* Vestris, dressed for her part in *Giovanni in London*, wearing revealing, tight-fitting breeches on her famous legs.

She also wore a red coat, embroidered and glittering, which reached down on her hips, although somehow it did not make her appearance any more respectable.

It was with an effort that Alisa managed to stare at *Madame*'s face rather than the lower part of her body.

She was certainly very pretty, with large sparkling dark eyes and curly black hair. She looked Italian, but when she spoke it was with a French accent, and Alisa remembered that she had only returned to England from Paris the previous year.

"You 'ave brought me sometheeng from Mrs. Lulworth?" she asked.

Somewhat belatedly Alisa remembered that as a pedlar she should have curtseyed.

Hastily she replied:

"Yes, *Madame*. Mrs. Lulworth informed me that you require some new face-creams, and I have some very exceptional ones which have never been sold in London before."

"Can that be true?" *Madame* Vestris enquired.

Quickly Alisa opened her bag, and as she did so she looked round for something on which to stand it while she took out the contents.

Every available table in the dressing-room was piled with flowers, which were also ranged against the walls.

But as she looked behind her Alisa was aware that *Madame* was not alone, for there was a Gentleman she had not at first noticed, seated in a comfortable chair with his legs stretched out in front of him.

She only had a quick glance at him, and then, intent on what she had come for, she drew out the first pot.

"This is called *The Freshness of Spring*," she said.

"All the ingredients come from our garden, and it really does make the skin soft and removes all blemishes."

"I verry much doubt zat!" *Madame* Vestris replied cynically. "And who could 'elp haveeng a dry skeen in thees terrible climate?"

Feeling a little braver, Alisa said:

"May I suggest, *Madame*, that you use *The Freshness of Spring* at night, and once or twice a week use *Red Sunrise*, which contains carrots which clear the skin of any impurities."

Madame Vestris opened the pots and sniffed them.

Then, as if she looked at Alisa for the first time, she said:

"You speak as eef you know wat you talk about, but do you use these creams or are you just 'ired to sell them?"

Because what she said sounded rude, Alisa stiffened. Then she said:

"I promise you, *Madame*, I not only use them myself but I also make them. It was my mother who taught me how to mix the ingredients."

"Your skeen is certainly verry clear," *Madame* Vestris said grudgingly.

Now Alisa thought she was looking at her in a hostile manner, and she said quickly:

"In a month's time I shall be able to make a wonderful cream from fresh strawberries. It is extremely efficacious for very bad eruptions or spots."

"I do not 'ave the spots!" *Madame* Vestris said sharply, and for the moment Alisa thought she had offended her.

Holding the pots of *The Freshness of Spring* and *Red Sunrise* in her hands, *Madame* took them to the dressing-table on which Alisa could see a huge array of bottles and pots.

There was also a hare's foot, rouge, brushes and pencils for the eye-brows, as well as innumerable sticks of grease-paint.

She could not help looking at everything with interest.

Then she forced herself to watch *Madame* Vestris, who, sitting down, had begun to smooth some *Red Sunrise* on one cheek and *The Freshness of Spring* on the other.

"I wonder eef these are any different from the ones I 'ave tried before?" she remarked.

"I promise you they are," Alisa insisted, "and after using them for one night you will notice an improvement."

"Eet ees not the creams that impress me so much as your skeen," *Madame* Vestris said. "I cannot 'elp thinking that either you are the best recommendation a product ever 'ad, or else you are such a good actress that you should be on the boards!"

"Perhaps she is both!" a drawling voice said from behind them.

For the moment Alisa had forgotten that there was someone else there, and, as if *Madame* Vestris had forgotten too, she turned a laughing face towards the Gentleman.

"Advise me, *Milor',*" she said. "Shall I try something new?"

"It is something you have never been backward in doing in the past," the Gentleman replied, and *Madame* Vestris laughed again.

"*C'est vrai,* and when I'm daring, I 'ave never regretted it."

"Why should you, when you have taken London by storm?" the Gentleman asked.

Alisa was aware that they were speaking of *Madame's* daring act of appearing as a man in the very debatable breeches.

She glanced down at them and thought it was in fact very brave of any woman to appear on stage in such outrageous garb.

Then as *Madame* rubbed the cream into her cheeks
and powdered them she asked:

"How much is that charlatan Mrs. Lulworth expecting
me to pay for thees? I'm quite certain 'twill be sometheeng
extraordinaire!"

Alisa drew in her breath, but before she could speak,
Madame Vestris went on:

"I'm quite aware that eef I use them, by tomorrow all
London will follow my example, so really I should be
paid for introducing a new fashion and not 'ave to put
my 'and into my own pocket!"

Alisa felt with a sudden stab of horror that if *Madame*
refused to pay, Mrs. Lulworth would certainly not buy
them from her.

Then the drawling voice said:

"I suggest you leave that to me. As you are well
aware, Lucy, I am quite prepared to be your Banker."

Madame Vestris laughed.

"It would certainly be an original present, and very
much cheaper than a diamond bracelet."

"Is that what you want?"

Madame Vestris shrugged her shoulders in a typically
French gesture.

"What woman ever has enough diamonds?" she asked
softly.

"I will not forget," the Gentleman said. "Now,
regrettably, I must leave you, but tonight I will collect
you after the Show, and I promise you will not be
disappointed with the party that has been arranged in
your honour."

"In which case I must certainly use your latest present, *Milor'*."

The Gentleman walked to the dressing-table and
Alisa was aware that he was tall and broad-shouldered.

He was also extremely elegantly dressed, and she
appreciated the high polish on his Hessian boots and
the intricate way in which his crisp white cravat was tied.

She knew only too well how difficult it was to achieve such perfection, for she had helped her father with his cravats. He was always too impatient and kept saying: "That will do! That will do!" long before she was satisfied.

She moved her eyes from the Gentleman's cravat to his face, and she thought he was extremely handsome if somewhat overpowering.

Something in his firm features, strongly marked eyebrows, and square chin made Alisa aware that he had a dominating character and perhaps even an aggressive one.

At the same time, she looked at him curiously, thinking that perhaps he was the type of gentleman whom Penelope might meet in London.

Then she told herself that he was too old for Penelope and anyway she had no wish for her sister to be pursued by the type of men who were enamoured of actresses and Opera-dancers.

Although they lived very quietly in the country, reports of the excesses introduced by the Prince Regent had gradually percolated through to the village, and they talked with bated breath of the Prince of Wales's association with Mrs. Fitzherbert and then with Lady Jersey, who was followed in turn by Lady Hertford.

They were only names to Alisa, but when she listened to the conversation of her father and some of his friends, they kept cropping up, and Eloise and her mother, Mrs. Kingston, were always full of the latest gossip whenever they returned from a visit to London.

The Bucks and Beaux, Alisa learnt, pursued pretty actresses and women whom no lady would condescend to know.

Now as the Gentleman raised *Madame* Vestris's hand to his lips, Alisa told herself that she would have to take great care that Penelope did not become involved in any way with Rakes or the sort of men who would flirt with her without intending to offer marriage.

"Until tonight," the Gentleman said.

Then, looking at Alisa, he said:

"Come with me, I will settle your account."

Alisa was just about to ask why she should go with him when there was a sudden loud knock on the door and a voice called:

"On stage, *Madame!*"

Madame Vestris gave a little cry, and, snatching up a plumed hat that was lying on a chair near some flowers, said:

"*Au revoir, Milor'*. I look forward to—*tonight.*"

She accentuated the last word and gave him what Alisa felt was a very intimate glance from under her mascaraed eye-lashes.

Then she was gone and they could hear her footsteps hurrying along the passage towards the stage.

Alisa looked up and found that the Gentleman was staring at her in a penetrating manner which made her feel shy.

"As I imagine you have no carriage," he said in the dry, somewhat drawling manner in which apparently he always spoke, "I will convey you wherever you wish to go."

"There is no need," Alisa said quickly. "I walked here . . . and I can walk back."

"From where?"

"From Bond Street."

"As I live in Berkeley Square, we go in the same direction, and I think you will find my Phaeton quicker than your feet."

It seemed rather foolish to protest, and Alisa therefore said quietly:

"Thank you."

She walked out through the door first, and as she did

so she was conscious that beside the Gentleman's elegant appearance she must look very shabby and insignificant.

They reached the old man who was seated once more in his glass box, and as they passed him Alisa thought he smiled at her.

"Thank you very much!" she said, and then she and the Gentleman went out through the door.

Outside the stage-door, which was in a side-street, there was a magnificent pair of horses and a Phaeton which was higher and more splendid than any vehicle Alisa had ever seen before in her life.

Yellow and black, it seemed to shine like its owner's Hessian boots.

She stood staring first at the horses, then at the Phaeton, until the Gentleman said with a slight smile:

"I am waiting to help you!"

"I am sorry," she said humbly, and put her hand in his.

He helped her up onto the seat, then went round to the other side to take the reins from his groom, who climbed into the small seat at the back behind the hood.

As the horses moved away, Alisa thought that never again in her whole life would she drive in anything so smart and so impressive.

'Penelope will be very envious!' she thought.

"I am interested to know what you are thinking," a voice said beside her.

"I was thinking how magnificent your horses are," Alisa replied, "and your Phaeton is finer than any vehicle I have ever seen!"

She wondered if she should add that she had never before driven behind horses which wore a harness of real silver.

"I am gratified by your appreciation," the Gentleman said, "but at the same time I am mortified that you have not referred to the driver of such a turn-out."

For a moment Alisa did not know what he meant. Then quickly, without thinking, she replied:

"Mama always said it was very rude to make personal remarks."

The Gentleman laughed.

"You are not as demure as you appear."

"I hope not," Alisa replied, thinking how shabby and nondescript she looked.

"What do you mean by that?"

For a moment she wondered if she should tell him the truth, then decided that there was no reason not to do so.

"I had to come to London ... alone, and I had no wish to be ... noticed."

There was just a little tremor on the last word, as she remembered the man who had tried to speak to her in Bond Street.

"That was certainly wise," the Gentleman replied. "I gather you live in the country, where you make these miraculous products to sell to famous actresses."

He made it sound rather a dreary pursuit, Alisa thought, and she decided it would be a mistake to answer, so she merely looked ahead of her, holding her chin a little higher than she had done before.

"I was just thinking," the Gentleman went on, "that as I have to drive first to my house to write a cheque to pay you for your wares, perhaps you would like to join me for luncheon before you continue your sales or return to the country."

As he finished speaking, Alisa was aware that she was in fact very hungry.

She was quite certain that by now it was past noon, which was the hour Mrs. Brigstock usually gave them luncheon, and it was a long time since she had eaten an egg for her breakfast.

She had in fact been too excited and too afraid of

missing the Stage-Coach to eat any more even if it had been provided.

Now she was conscious of what was an emptiness inside her, and the idea of luncheon of any sort was very attractive.

"It is very . . . kind of you to suggest it," she said hesitatingly, "but I do not . . . wish to be a . . . bother in any . . . way."

"You will certainly not be that," the Gentleman answered. "And I imagine that you would not wish to spend much of the money I am paying you on food, which in London is quite expensive."

"No, indeed not!" Alisa said quickly. "The money is for . . . something very . . . special. But perhaps it would be . . . best for me to wait to eat until I arrive home."

As she spoke, she thought that if she had to do that, she would be ravenously hungry.

But she had no idea where she could buy anything to eat and she was sure that her father would be very angry at the idea of her eating alone in a public place.

"You will have luncheon with me," the Gentleman said firmly, "and you can tell me about yourself. I am interested in how you make your creams, and why."

It flashed through Alisa's mind that he might be thinking of buying some himself. Then she thought that was a ridiculous idea.

There was a lot of traffic about and the Gentleman did not speak again until they were driving down Albemarle Street.

"Do you often come to London?" he asked.

Alisa shook her head.

"I have not been here for two years," she replied, "and there appear to be more carriages on the roads than there was then. But of course it is Coronation Year."

"That is undoubtedly the explanation," the Gentleman replied, "and at this rate of increase, the whole of the traffic in London will inevitably come to a stand-still!"

Alisa laughed, for it seemed a funny idea. Then the horses were drawn up outside a very large and impressive house at the end of the Square.

She remembered seeing it once before and thinking how attractive it looked.

Over the front door was a portico supported by two pillars, and the moment the horses came to a stop, footmen in powdered wigs laid down a red carpet so that Alisa stepped from the Phaeton onto it.

She waited until the Gentleman had walked round from the other side of the Phaeton to join her. Then they walked into a large, cool Hall in which there was an impressive staircase and a number of paintings in gilded frames.

"We have a guest for luncheon, Dawkins," the Gentleman said to the Butler, "and I expect the young lady would like to go upstairs."

"Yes, M'Lord."

A gesture of the Butler's hand made a footman come to Alisa's side to say:

"Will you please follow me, Miss."

Obediently she went up the staircase, feeling that because the carpet was so thick and soft her feet sank into it.

'This is an adventure!' she thought. "I must notice and remember everything so that I can tell Penelope.'

She was shown into a bedroom on the first floor which was more magnificent than any other room she had ever seen.

There was brocade on the walls, a draped bed, fringed curtains, and a dressing-table with a muslin flounce trimmed with lace. She looked round wide-eyed until a housemaid came hurrying into the room.

"I've come to help you, Miss," she said.

Alisa took off her cloak, then sat down at the pretty dressing-table to remove her bonnet.

There were gold-backed hair-bushes and a comb, also edged with gold, with which to tidy her hair.

She was glad that she had washed it only yesterday, so that its natural wave fell gracefully on each side of her face, and she knew that while she might not look smart, she was certainly tidy.

Her gown of deep blue seemed to accentuate the whiteness of her skin, and she thought gratefully that it was that which had really sold the pots of cream first to Mrs. Lulworth and then to *Madame* Vestris.

She remembered excitedly that both these women had said there would be a demand for more, and she began to calculate how many pots she and Penelope could make before they went to stay with Aunt Harriet.

She hoped that if *Madame* Vestris was pleased, Mrs. Lulworth would allow them at least one gown on credit, and although Penelope might say that two of them together were more impressive than one, Penelope must go to the first parties.

Only when they could afford a second gown would she, Alisa, be able to join her sister.

The housemaid was carrying across the room a shining brass can filled with hot water which somebody had handed through the door.

Now she poured the water into a basin which Alisa noticed was made of very pretty flowered china with a ewer to match, which stood in the corner.

She washed her hands and face and felt fresher and free of the dust which had blown out behind the Stage-Coach in a huge cloud.

Then as she dried her hands she said:

"Thank you very much for helping me. When I go downstairs, will there be somebody to show me where I am to go?"

"Yes, of course, Miss," the maid replied. "Mr. Dawkins, the Butler, will be waiting for you."

She spoke as if for him to fail to do so would be a social error, and Alisa smiled.

She tried to remember all the things her mother had told her about grand houses and what happened when one stayed in them.

She hoped she would not make a lot of mistakes when, as Penelope hoped and prayed, they were invited to parties of any consequence.

She wondered if the Gentleman who was being so kind as to give her luncheon would be of any help, then once again she felt certain that he was not the type of person with whom she would wish her sister to associate.

The Butler, waiting at the foot of the stairs, led her without speaking to a door at the end of the Hall.

When she entered the room, Alisa saw that it was a Library painted a deep shade of green and picked out in gold with books set into every wall.

There was shelf after shelf of them, and she could not help giving a little exclamation of excitement before she turned her eyes to her host, who was standing in front of the fireplace waiting for her.

"What a beautiful Library!" she said. "You are lucky to have so many books!"

There was a faint smile on his rather hard mouth before he replied:

"It is a possession on which I do not usually receive many congratulations."

"Why not?" Alisa asked in surprise, as she moved towards him.

"I find that few people have time to read, and women are certainly not among them."

"How extraordinary!" Alisa exclaimed.

She was genuinely surprised. Her father was always reading and so was she, and in the Library at home her mother had had a whole section in which she kept her favourite books.

"I suppose from that remark I must assume you are a reader?" the Gentleman asked.

"But of course!" Alisa replied.

"Before we express our opinions on this or any other subject, let me offer you a glass of champagne, or would you prefer madeira?"

Alisa hesitated.

She was very tempted to accept champagne, which she had drunk only a few times in her life on special occasions, such as a birthday or Christmas, but then she remembered that she had eaten nothing for a long time.

"I think," she said after a little pause, "I should say 'no.'"

"Why?"

His monosyllabic question, spoken in a dry, abrupt manner, was, Alisa thought, almost intimidating.

"I had breakfast a long time ago."

"So you are being sensible. Is that something you invariably are? Or do you just consider it advisable on this particular occasion?"

Alisa considered the question for a moment.

"I hope I am always sensible."

"Then as this is the exception rather than the rule, I suggest I give you a very little champagne just to celebrate our first meeting."

Alisa thought it was rather a strange thing to say.

At the same time, because he spoke so impersonally and in the same tone of voice he had used before, she thought it was just a manner of speaking, rather than that they actually had anything to celebrate.

He took the champagne bottle from the gold ice-bucket and poured her a small glass of it, which he then handed to her.

As she took it she said:

"It may seem rather a belated question . . . but could you please . . . tell me . . . your name?"

"I forgot we had not introduced ourselves. I am the Earl of Keswick.* Now inform me who you are."

"I am Alisa Wyn . . ."

As she spoke, Alisa suddenly remembered that if they were to be coming to London and, as Penelope hoped, be acclaimed for their beauty, it would be a great mistake for anybody to know how they had been able to buy their gowns, least of all this cynical and imperious man.

" . . . Winter," she finished. "Alisa Winter."

"The name does not suit you," the Earl replied, "at least not the second part of it. But 'Alisa' is charming, and I do not think I have ever known anybody by that name before."

"It is Greek."

"Who told you that?"

"I have always known it, I imagine because my mother was very interested in Greek Mythology."

She thought the Earl raised his eye-brows, but at that moment the Butler announced:

"Luncheon is served, M'Lord."

Alisa took another sip of the champagne, then because she thought it was wise not to drink any more she put it down on a table.

Then she walked ahead of the Earl and as she stepped into the Hall she saw that the maid who had looked after her upstairs was putting her cloak and bonnet on a chair, together with the black bag which had contained her pots.

It made Alisa remember that she must not take too long over luncheon. She must give herself time to go

---

*(pronounced Kes-ick)

back to Bond Street to tell Mrs. Lulworth what had occurred, and then she must hurry to the *Two-Headed Swan* in Islington.

If she missed the Coach it would be disastrous!

The Dining-Room was a delightful room, oval in shape and painted in what Alisa knew was a pale Adam green, with alcoves in which stood statues of Greek gods and goddesses.

As she sat down in the place indicated to her, she looked at them excitedly and said:

"I wonder if I can guess who each statue represents. I am sure the one opposite me is Apollo."

"You are right," the Earl said. "But before we start talking once again of my possessions, I suggest you tell me about yourself, Miss Winter."

He frowned, then he said:

"No! 'Winter' is wrong! You must be 'Alisa.' It is a lovely name and it suits you."

Alisa was hardly attending to what he was saying, knowing that it would be a great mistake for him to know too much about her.

Then she thought that her fears were probably groundless.

Contrary to Penelope's plan of getting in touch with the Marchioness of Conyngham, she had the unhappy feeling they would end up sewing for the natives in Africa and copying out tracts. And Aunt Harriet's complaints about the wickedness of the world would force them to go to Church at least half-a-dozen times a week.

'If only we could stay in a house like this!' she thought wistfully.

Then as she started to eat she realised how hungry she was, and she knew that the food was more delicious than anything she had ever tasted before.

The Earl sent away the red wine which the Butler had offered and had it replaced by white. By the time he spoke, Alisa had eaten half of what was on her place.

"I am waiting!" he remarked.

"There is . . . nothing to tell," Alisa said quickly, "unless you want to hear about country life, like the arrival of the cuckoo, the first baby lamb born in the field next to the garden, and the loveliness of the daffodils which of course grow wild."

She spoke in the teasing way that she would have spoken to Penelope, and after a moment the Earl said:

"What *Madame* Vestris said about you is right. You are in fact a consummate and extremely skilful actress."

"If I were, I would then be able to make a great deal of money," Alisa replied. "I remember reading in a newspaper that *Madame* Vestris receives an enormous salary every week, and her benefits exceed everybody else's."

"So that is what you want," the Earl remarked. "Money!"

"Not much," Alisa answered, "just enough for something very, very special which would make my sister very happy."

"And what is that?"

Alisa realised she had been indiscreet and wondered if in fact the champagne was making her talk too much.

"It is a secret, My Lord," she said. "And now please tell me about yourself. I have never seen such a beautiful house or so many treasures."

"Especially my books?"

"I noticed your paintings also as I went up the stairs."

"Then what shall we talk about?" the Earl enquired.

"It is difficult to decide what is the most important. When I look at the books we have at home, I shall think of those here, and the same applies to your paintings."

"And where is home?"

"It is just a small village in Hertfordshire. I do not think you will have heard of it."

"In other words, you are reluctant to tell me. Why should you be so secretive?"

"May I, in turn, My Lord, ask you why you are so inquisitive?"

"I should have thought the answer to that was obvious."

He realised that she looked puzzled, and he said:

"I have been looking at you and wondering how you make your skin so clear that it is almost transparent, and yet it seems to have the texture of a rose-petal."

Again, the dry way in which he spoke made it sound like something he was reading out of a book, rather than like a compliment, and Alisa laughed.

"Why are you laughing?" he demanded.

"Because I have never been told I am like a rose before. It is my sister who is always compared with a rose. I am a violet . . . an unimportant, quite unobtrusive little violet."

"For which one must search amongst the green leaves," the Earl said.

"You sound almost poetical, My Lord!"

"You will find quite a number of books of poetry in my Library."

Alisa gave a little sigh.

"I wish I could read every one of them, but Papa does not care for poetry and so we have very few at home."

The Earl helped himself to another course before he asked:

"You say you do not often stay in London?"

"Only very occasionally, although we may do so in the near future."

"To sell your creams?"

"Yes . . . of course," Alisa agreed quickly.

"It seems rather a dreary existence for a young girl to live in the country where nature is the only entertainment and to produce creams in order to make other women beautiful."

"I do hope that *Madame* Vestris will... like them."

Now there was a note of anxiety in Alisa's voice, as she thought how disappointed Penelope would be if after all their plans they had to come to London in the gowns they had made themselves and nobody would take any inerest in them.

It flashed through her mind that just one of the silver ornaments that decorated the table, just one of the silver dishes in which the food was served, would buy them half-a-dozen beautiful gowns in which, like the Misses Gunning, they would be a sensation.

"Oh, please... please God," she prayed silently, "let *Madame* Vestris find that the creams improve her skin."

She was praying with such intensity that she was startled when the Earl asked:

"Who are you thinking about?"

"*Madame* Vestris."

"You admire her?"

"I am... told she is a very... successful... actress."

"That is not what I asked you. When you first came into her dressing-room I thought that you were shocked by her appearance."

"I am... sure it was... presumptuous of me," Alisa said in a low voice, "but I did... think it was rather... immodest."

"Of course it is," the Earl agreed, "and that is why *Giovanni in London*, which is a very poor Show, is packed night after night."

"*Madame* Vestris has, I believe... a good... contralto voice."

"The public is more interested in her legs."

As the Earl spoke somewhat scathingly, Alisa blushed.

It seemed improper to be openly discussing another woman's legs.

"When you come to London," he said, "you will find that you have to move with the times. So perhaps it would be a mistake for you to come."

"A . . . mistake?" Alisa repeated.

"You would doubtless soon have your pretty head turned and become conceited, pleased with yourself, and ready to show off."

"I think that is a very unkind thing to say," Alisa replied. "I am sure I would become nothing of the sort! Anyway, I am not likely to receive any compliments."

As she spoke, she thought that the Missionaries and Parsons with whom Aunt Harriet concerned herself would certainly not be complimentary, if they noticed her at all.

"If you are not listening to compliments," the Earl said, "what will you be doing?"

"Sewing clothes for the natives for the Missionaries to take with them to Africa."

The Earl stared at her as if he could hardly believe what she was saying.

Then, as if she felt she had been wrong to be so frank, Alisa said quickly:

"There is no reason for you to be interested, My Lord. And please . . . as I must leave in a very short time, may I have one more look at your books?"

"Of course," the Earl agreed.

Alisa realised that the Butler was bringing a decanter of port to the table, and she said quickly:

"Forgive me! You have not finished, and it is very impolite of me to hurry you away when you have been so kind."

"I have finished," the Earl said, "and as I have no wish for any port, we will go to the Library and look at my books."

Feeling that she had been rather rude, Alisa rose and walked a little nervously ahead of him towards the Dining-Room door.

She remembered the way back to the Library, and as she entered the room the sunshine was coming through the windows, seeming to envelop everything with its golden light and make it part of a fairy-story.

The books in their leather covers tooled with gold against the green walls made a picture which she wished she could paint on canvass.

Over the mantelpiece, instead of the usual mirror, there was a very fine picture of horses which, although she was too shy to say so, she thought had been painted by Stubbs.

She stood looking round and realised that the Earl had walked to the desk that was in front of one of the windows and had sat down.

She thought he would not mind her roaming round, and as she read the titles of the books she realised that they were far more recent in publication than anything in her father's Library. His books were mostly historical and dealt with such ancient times that the peoples and nations they described were now extinct.

The Earl had a number of books on fascinating subjects which she wished she had time to read, but she moved on quickly, not wanting to miss anything, and saw that there was one shelf filled with books of poems, many of them by Lord Byron.

"Do you know Lord Byron?" she asked.

"Of course!" the Earl replied.

"I would love to have met him when he was in England."

"All women found him irresistibly attractive," the Earl replied, and she thought he spoke cynically.

"I was thinking not of his looks but of the way he wrote. There seems to be a feeling of life and excitement in his poetry which is irresistibly infectious. It makes me want to dance and sing and express myself in verse."

"I am sure George Byron would be very flattered by your appraisal of him," the Earl remarked.

He rose from the desk and Alisa turned from the book-shelves.

"Thank you for letting me look at your books," she said. "I feel almost as if I have stepped inside some of them, and listened to music."

The Earl held out an envelope, then he said:

"Here is the money I owe you."

"But . . . I have not told you how much the pots . . . cost."

"I think you will find the sum adequate, and now before you go I have something to suggest to you."

Alisa looked up at him and thought there was a rather strange expression in the Earl's eyes as he looked at her.

"I learnt, from all you have told me," he said, "that you are wasting your youth and certainly your beauty on the birds, the lambs, and the flowers, and I have a suggestion to make which I hope you will consider when you return home."

"A . . . suggestion?"

"It is that you let me look after you and give you all the things which will make you even lovelier than you are at the moment."

Alisa looked at him in a puzzled fashion, and he went on:

"Perhaps we could arrange it so that you can come to London without your family asking too many questions, but being content to know that you will be comfortable and well off."

"How . . . could I be? I do not know . . . what you are . . . suggesting."

The Earl smiled.

"I am suggesting that I will make you very happy and provide you with a fitting background. Or, should I say, a violet should not be hidden away so completely—at least not from me!"

As Alisa tried to understand what he was saying,

thinking that she must be very stupid to find it so difficult, the Earl's arms went round her.

Then before she could understand or realise what was happening, he had pulled her close to him, and as she looked up in astonishment his lips came down on hers.

For a moment she was paralysed into immobility by sheer surprise.

Then as she knew that she was being kissed for the first time in her life and that she should be horrified and shocked that anything so appalling should happen, she was aware of the strength of the Earl's arms, and the insistence of his lips, and a feeling that was different from anything she had ever felt before.

It was as if a wave of sunlight moved up through her body and into her breasts, to her throat, and then to her lips.

It was strange, yet at the same time, in a way she could not even grasp, it was so wonderful and rapturous that it was impossible to do anything but let it happen.

Her mind had ceased to function and all she was aware of was an ecstasy she had never known before in her whole life.

Then, as if suddenly she came out of a dream, she realised that she was in a strange man's arms and he was kissing her!

She knew it was the most shocking and reprehensible thing that could possibly happen!

She came back to reality and pressed her hands against the Earl's chest, and as his arms slackened she fought herself free with a sudden strength that he had not expected.

Then with a cry that echoed round the room she ran away from him, pulled open the door, and rushed across the Hall.

With a detached part of her mind she was aware that

her bonnet, cloak and bag were lying on a chair and she picked them up.

The front door was open, as a footman was taking a note from a groom in a livery.

As quickly as her legs could carry her, Alisa ran past them and up the Square until she saw a turning, then ran down another street to turn again into a Mews.

Only when with some detached part of her mind she knew it would be difficult for anybody to follow her did she stop running, breathless and with her heart pounding, beside the blank wall of a house.

She propped herself against it, shut her eyes, and told herself that it could not have happened and she must have been dreaming.

Chapter Three

"And after you had luncheon, what happened?"
Penelope insisted.

As she spoke, she thought that her sister looked very
pale and the long day in London had been too much for
her.

Penelope had met her sister at the crossroads, and
Alisa had been silent all the time they were walking
back through the village.

Only now, after she had washed and changed, was
she able to tell Penelope what had happened when she
visited Mrs. Lulworth's shop in Bond Street.

Penelope had listened entranced as Alisa described
how she had gone to the dressing-Room at the King's
Theatre to show *Madame* Vestris the pots of cream and
how the Gentleman she was entertaining had said he
would pay for them and had taken her back to his house
in Berkeley Square.

She had described the Dining-Room and the Library,
but now her voice trailed away into silence....

Alisa had decided on the way home in the Stage-
Coach that she must never, never tell Penelope that she
had been kissed.

It was something so reprehensible, so immodest on
her part, that she was desperately ashamed of her own
behaviour.

Yet, she was aware that she had to make some

explanation as to why, instead of returning to Mrs. Lulworth's shop as she should have done, she had gone directly, almost running, to the Two-Headed Swan in Islington. When she got there she had sat in the Waiting-Room, feeling that she must make herself invisible until she could board the Stage-Coach for her return journey.

In the Coach it had been difficult to think of anything but her own misbehaviour, and as she thought of it she felt again that strange feeling of rapture and wonder that the Earl's lips had evoked in her.

'I had no idea that being kissed could make me feel like that,' she thought, and blushed because it was impossible not to be shocked at herself.

What would her mother have said if she had known that Alisa had allowed a strange man whom she had met for the first time to put his arms round her and touch her?

But she had to make some explanation to Penelope, and, apart from the kiss, she thought she must tell the truth.

"What happened, Alisa?" Penelope asked again.

"I hardly . . . like to . . . tell you."

"Are you trying to say that he made love to you?"

"N-not . . . exactly."

"Then what did happen?"

Alisa looked down at her clasped hands.

"He suggested that he should . . . look after me so that I should . . . not have to . . . work and sell . . . face-creams."

To her surprise, Penelope gave a cry that was not exactly one of disapproval.

"Oh, poor Alisa!" she exclaimed. "But of course it is what you might have expected from going to luncheon alone with a man in his house."

Alisa raised her head to look at her sister wide-eyed.

"Do you . . . think it was . . . wrong of me?"

"It is what I would have done in the circumstances, rather than go hungry, but of course it made him think you were not a lady."

Alisa groaned.

"How could I have been so . . . foolish? But he seemed so . . . aloof and not the . . . type of man who would . . . behave in such an . . . ungentlemanly fashion."

Penelope laughed.

"It has nothing to do with being a gentleman, and Eloise says that all the gentlemen in London have mistresses who are either actresses, dancers, or pretty Cyprians. For them it is much the same as owning good horse-flesh."

Alisa jumped to her feet.

"How can you know such . . . things?" she demanded. "And if you do . . . why have you not . . . told me?"

"Because, dearest, you would have been horrified, you know you would! No lady would speak of such women, but it proves how lovely we both are, and even in your drab, old-fashioned clothes the Earl was attracted to you."

Alisa drew in her breath and hoped that Penelope would not guess that because he was attracted to her he had kissed her.

Aloud she said:

"It is . . . something I do not take as a . . . compliment, and I have no . . . wish to . . . speak about it again."

"No, of course not," Penelope said soothingly. "You must just forget, dearest, that you were frightened, and remember that your visit to London has been completely and overwhelmingly successful."

Alisa looked at her in a startled fashion.

"You mean we must go . . . back to . . . Mrs. Lulworth and sell her . . . more face-creams?"

"But of course!" Penelope said. "If, as you say, the

mere fact that *Madame* Vestris is using them will make everybody demand the same creams, then the sooner we get to work, the better!"

Alisa wanted to cry out that she could not do it and never again would she go to Mrs. Lulworth's shop or anywhere else where she might meet the Earl.

Before she could speak, Penelope said:

"Dearest, do you not see how wonderful this is? We can have the gowns we wanted, and then we can write to the Marchioness of Conyngham. I know in my very bones that we are going to be just as successful as Maria and Elizabeth Gunning."

It flashed through Alisa's mind that Maria had married an Earl, but she told herself that marriage was the very last thing the Earl of Keswick was likely to offer her.

'I must forget him,' she thought to herself, and tried to listen to Penelope as she went on excitedly:

"I am sure you were right when you said Mrs. Lulworth might give us credit to have the four essential gowns we need before we can pay for them completely. How much did the Earl give you?"

"Three pounds, I suppose."

"Where is it?" Penelope asked, as if she wished to look at it and make sure there was no mistake.

"He wrote a cheque," Alisa replied. "It is in my silk bag in which I took the pots to London. I left it in the Hall."

"I will fetch it."

Penelope left the Sitting-Room and came back a moment later with the bag in her hand.

"We must start work first thing tomorrow," she was saying. "I noticed there were three cucumbers ready for picking in the garden this morning, and I will send one of the village boys to collect some watercress down by the mill."

As she was speaking she had taken the envelope out of Alisa's bag, and now as she opened it she gave a shrill scream.

"What is it? What is the matter?" Alisa asked.

Her sister was staring at the cheque she held in her hand as if she could not believe her eyes.

"What is wrong, Penelope?"

"Nothing is wrong," Penelope answered, and her voice suddenly sounded hoarse. "Do you know how much this cheque is for?"

"I thought it would be for three pounds."

"It is for fifty!"

"I do not believe it!"

Alisa walked to her sister's side and took the cheque from her hands.

Penelope was right. The cheque, made out to "Miss Alisa Winter" in a strong, upright hand, was for fifty pounds.

"There must be some . . . mistake," she said in a whisper. "I will tear it up."

Penelope snatched the cheque from her.

"You will do nothing of the sort!"

"But we cannot keep it."

"Why not?"

"Because it would be stealing."

"He gave it to you."

Alisa thought for a moment. Then she said in a halting tone:

"I suppose . . . because he thought I would . . . agree to what he . . . suggested . . ."

"Well, he will be disappointed, but I for one am grateful to him."

"But we . . . cannot take the . . . money!"

"I do not see why not."

"Because it is . . . something nobody with any . . . breeding or . . . decency would do."

"He was not giving it to you because he thought you were well-bred or decent, but because he thought you were lovely, which you are, Alisa."

"I have no . . . intention of . . . behaving like the woman he . . . thought me to be," Alisa said proudly.

"Well, I have no such qualms," Penelope replied. "Think, Alisa! This is the answer to our prayers. We can have the gowns we want, the bonnets to go with them, and there will be no difficulty now about obtaining everything else on credit."

"I will not . . . let you . . . keep it," Alisa said fiercely.

"Then you must write to the Earl, explain who you are, and ask him to apologise."

"You . . . know I . . . cannot do . . . that."

"Then why make such a fuss?"

Penelope, looking at her sister's face, realised that she was really upset, and she said in a very different tone of voice:

"Please, Alisa dearest, be sensible for my sake. This is a gift from the gods, and it is fate that we should receive it at this particular moment when we need it so badly. How can you be so ungrateful?"

"It is not a question of . . . gratitude," Alisa said, "but of . . . conscience."

Penelope paused for a moment, then in her most persuasive voice she said:

"You went to London to help me. How can you be so unkind and so cruel as to make me go and stay with Aunt Harriet looking like I am now? Nobody will be interested in me, unless of course I am so fortunate, as you were, to find unexpectedly a stranger who is prepared to spend a great deal of money on me."

Alisa looked at her sister in a startled fashion.

"You are not to . . . think of such . . . things!"

"It happened to you. Why should it not happen to me?" Penelope asked. "And I should certainly have no scruples about taking everything I could get."

She saw that she had horrified Alisa, but she went on:

"To the Earl, the loss of fifty pounds is like backing a horse which does not win. It is bad luck, but he will merely shrug his shoulders and not think of it again."

Alisa walked to the window but outside she did not see the daffodils and the almond-blossoms.

Instead, she saw Penelope growing more bitter and frustrated and perhaps in consequence getting into trouble. She did not try to explain to herself what that trouble might be.

But it was difficult not to remember the strength of the Earl's arms and how his lips had taken possession of her so that it was impossible to move and she could no longer think.

As if she knew that Alisa was weakening; Penelope got up and joined her at the window and put her arms round her.

"Please, please, Alisa," she begged, "do not spoil things for me. If we can have just a month or even two weeks in London wearing beautiful gowns, I am sure everything in our lives will somehow be changed."

"I do not . . . know what to . . . say," Alisa said unhappily.

"Then leave everything to me," Penelope said, "and if it worries you so very much, why do you not send the Earl a present?"

"A . . . present?"

"Well, there must be something in the house that he would like, and therefore you need not feel so guilty about taking his money."

Alisa thought of the Earl's paintings, his books, the silver on the table, and the gold ice-bucket from which he had poured her out a glass of champagne.

It was almost laughable to think that anything they possessed would have the slightest interest for him.

Then, almost as if something outside herself made

her think of it, she remembered the painting which hung in her father's bedroom.

She had painted it after he had called Penelope and herself "The Rose and the Violet."

It had been spring, and she had gone out into the garden to pick a bunch of the first white violets peeping from between their green leaves.

It had taken a great deal of patience to paint them, but when she had finished the picture, both her mother and her father had said it was the best painting she had ever done.

"You must think of me whenever you look at it," Alisa had told her father.

"I would rather look at you, my darling," he had replied.

Nevertheless, her mother had found a pretty carved and gilded wooden frame for Alisa to put her painting in, and they had hung it on the wall in her father's bedroom.

She was sure her father would not miss it, but she told herself that she would paint him another exactly the same in case he should ask where the original had gone.

"If I send the Earl a . . . present," she said aloud, "he might know where it had come from."

"You can give it to Fred, the Carrier," Penelope replied. "He goes to London every week, and he is so stupid he is not likely to ask any questions."

There was a light in her eyes and a smile on her lips because she knew she had won and Alisa would now agree to keep the fifty pounds.

"We will put the money in the Bank when we get to London," she said aloud, "because we would not want Mrs. Lulworth to know that the Earl had given you the money to pay her."

"No, of course not," Alisa said quickly. Then she added:

"Supposing . . . because I would not do what he . . . suggested, that he . . . stops the . . . cheque?"

She remembered how once her father had stopped a cheque because he found he had paid the same bill twice.

"That would leave three pots of cream unpaid for," Penelope said quickly, "and I cannot believe that any gentleman would behave so meanly."

"No. I am . . . sure you are . . . right," Alisa agreed.

She was thinking that whatever she felt about his behaviour, at least the Earl was a man of honour.

She did not know why she was so sure, but she was, and she thought too that Penelope was right when she said that losing fifty pounds would be to him no more than backing a horse which lost a race.

Penelope kissed her cheek.

"Cheer up, dearest, you have been very, very clever. Now everything is going to be exciting and wonderful, and I am quite, quite sure that the Marchioness of Conyngham will help us."

She was so thrilled that she could talk of nothing else the whole evening, and she did not appear to notice that Alisa was very quiet.

When finally Alisa turned out the light and was alone in the darkness, she found it impossible to sleep.

All she could think of was the Earl, what they had said to each other at luncheon, and being held captive in a way which was more exciting and more marvellous than any dream she had ever had before.

"How could a kiss from a man I did not even know be so wonderful?" she asked herself not once but a dozen times before she finally fell asleep.

* * *

"Now that you are here," Lady Ledbury said, "I hope you are prepared to work. There is a great deal to be done."

"I am sorry, Aunt Harriet," Penelope replied, "but we will not be able to help you on this visit as much as we have been able to do in the past."

Lady Ledbury looked at her niece in astonishment.

Unlike her brother, even when she was young she had never been particularly good-looking, and with age she had grown gaunt and bony. With her greying hair dragged back from her forehead, and wearing an extremely ugly black gown, she looked rather like an aged raven.

"I do not know what you mean, Penelope!" she said sharply.

"Papa has given us instructions, now that we are grown up, as to how we are to employ our time in London," Penelope said airily. "And although we are very grateful to you for having us to stay, Aunt Harriet, Alisa and I will have to spend quite a lot of time on our own interests."

To say that Lady Ledbury was taken aback was to express it midly.

She had, in fact, although she would never have admitted it, looked forward to having her two nieces to stay so that they could help her with her Charities, and at the same time she would have somebody to order about and bully.

The servants in the house, who had been with her for a long time, had learnt that when she told them to do anything they thought was unnecessary, it was best to agree, and then to forget it or find there was no time to carry out her commands.

Because she paid them little and they were as it happened well trained, Lady Ledbury was aware that it would be a great mistake to push them so far that they would leave.

In the past, the help that Alisa and Penelope had given her had received the approval of her pet beneficiaries, which had been like music in her ears.

Only this morning she had said to the Vicar of St. Mary's, Islington:

"I know you have had difficulty recently, Vicar, in finding somebody to repair your hymn-books, but my nieces are coming to stay and they are quite skilful with their fingers, so that if you bring to me tomorrow the books that need repairing, I will make that one of their tasks while they are with me."

"How very kind of you, Lady Ledbury," the Vicar had answered. "It will be a great help, and I must make a point of bringing it to the attention of the Church Wardens at the next Vestry Meeting."

Now Lady Ledbury saw that her authority was being undermined, and she said quickly:

"I must make it clear from the beginning, Penelope, that I expect both you and Alisa to repay my hospitality by making yourselves useful."

"Perhaps that will be possible a little later, Aunt," Penelope answered in what her aunt thought was a very impertinent manner.

Lady Ledbury decided that somehow she would prevent this independent nonsense from going too far.

"Do be careful!" Alisa warned Penelope when they went upstairs to the small and comfortable but dull bedroom they always occupied.

"I am not afraid of Aunt Harriet!" Penelope replied. "And I am only praying that Mrs. Lulworth can fit us out very quickly with our new gowns, and we can then call on the Marchioness."

Alisa made a sound, but she did not argue, and Penelope had once again won a battle when it came to carrying out her plan of writing to her mother's old friend and saying that they had a memento for her.

"How can we possibly find anything that will be good enough?" Alisa asked.

"There must be something," Penelope said confidently.

Only after a great deal of searching and argument did

they find amongst her mother's things a pretty hand-
kerchief-sachet that Lady Wynton had embroidered
with her own monogram and trimmed with a piece of
real lace from one of her gowns when she had been a
girl.

"Do you not see!" Penelope exclaimed excitedly. "We
can say that Mama told us that when she wore that
particular gown she was staying with the Denisons, and
we felt sure that was why the Marchioness would like to
have it."

"How do you know that is true?" Alisa asked.

"I feel instinctively that it is," Penelope replied loftily.

Penelope was so excited at the idea of the new
gowns that she found it difficult to sleep the night after
they arrived at her aunt's house, while Alisa lay awake
worrying.

"Suppose," she asked herself, "the Marchioness does
ask us to her house, or even to a party, and I meet the
Earl. What will I say to him? How could I ever explain
that I spent his money when really I should have
returned it with a polite note saying that he made a
mistake and the price of the creams was exactly three
pounds?"

But, to do that, she would have to give him her name
and address, and although she was quite certain he had
forgotten her by now, there was just a chance, a very
slim one, that he might have wanted to see her again.

'I shall just have to pray,' she thought finally, 'that he
is too busy with *Madame* Vestris to wish to go to
respectable parties such as the Marchioness would give.'

                              *   *   *

The following morning, having breakfasted with their
aunt, Penelope managed to evade her questions as to
where they were going before they set off for Bond
Street.

"I do not know that I really approve of you walking

about London alone," Lady Ledbury had said in a last
effort to extract from them their destination once they
left her house.

"I always understood," Penelope replied, "that it was
correct for two ladies to walk about together and only if
a lady is alone should she be accompanied by a maid.
But of course, Aunt Harriet, if you want us to take one
of the housemaids, then we will do so."

Penelope knew as she spoke that not only were the
housemaids too old to walk far, but also it would be
difficult for her aunt to spare them from their usual
duties.

"I suppose you will be all right," Lady Ledbury
admitted grudgingly, and did not notice the glance of
amusement Penelope gave to Alisa.

It was a sunny spring day, and the two girls, walking
in what was actually a very countrified manner, reached
Bond Street even more quickly than Alisa had done
when she had come to London the previous week.

Because Penelope had for the moment no wish to
stare at other shops, being intent on only one thing—
for them to be elegantly dressed as swiftly as possible—she
walked straight towards the Piccadilly end of Bond
Street.

"Once we are well dressed," she said to Alisa, "we
can start being débutantes."

Alisa felt that her sister was being over-optimistic,
but, because she loved Penelope and wanted her to be
happy, she had no wish to damp down her enthusiasm.

They reached Mrs. Lulworth's shop and Penelope's
eyes were shining as just before they entered she
pointed out a very elegant bonnet in the window that
bore no resemblance whatsoever to those they had on
their heads.

The high crown was encircled with a wreath of
crimson roses and the pointed brim was edged with a
row of delicate lace.

"That is what we want," Penelope said firmly, and walked into the shop.

She asked for Mrs. Lulworth in an authoritative manner and a moment later they were facing the large, rather frightening woman whom Alisa had met before.

"How can I help you, young ladies?" Mrs. Lulworth began, then she looked at Alisa and gave a cry.

"Where have you been?" she enquired. "Why did you not come back to me as I expected you to do? It was only when you left that I realised I had not asked your name and had no idea how I could get in touch with you."

"Why did you wish to do so?" Penelope enquired, realising that Alisa had lost her voice.

"*Madame* Vestris was absolutely delighted with the face-cream. A number of other actresses have asked for them, and already the rumour has spread round those in Society that I have something new!"

"I see . . ." Penelope said slowly, "and so you need some more creams!"

As if she felt she had been too enthusiastic, Mrs. Lulworth answered warily:

"I might consider taking some more, of course on sale-or-return."

"I am afraid that would not suit us," Penelope answered. "We have a proposition to put to you, and perhaps we could sit down while I tell you what my sister and I have in our minds."

She was aware that Alisa was looking at her apprehensively, as if she thought she was being very high-handed, but Mrs. Lulworth merely said:

"Perhaps you would come into my private office where we'll not be disturbed."

"I think that would be a good idea," Penelope agreed.

As they followed Mrs. Lulworth, she squeezed Alisa's hand to reassure her.

Half-an-hour later they came back into the shop,

Mrs. Lulworth looking somewhat bewildered, at the same time treating what she now considered two customers in a very different manner.

Penelope had stated their terms very clearly:

They would give Mrs. Lulworth fifty pounds to provide them with gowns and other accessories which they needed immediately.

They had fifty pots of face-creams with them in London and would make more if necessary.

The fifty pots must be credited to them outright at ten shillings per pot.

There was a heated argument while Mrs. Lulworth insisted that seven shillings was all she could pay, while Penelope stuck to her figure of ten.

There was quite a battle before finally Penelope accepted nine shillings with the proviso that, if there was a sudden rush for more and they had to go to the country to make more cream, for the next batch they would receive ten shillings.

Alisa had taken no part in the discussion. She only thought that she would easily have been talked into accepting seven shillings with gratitude, and that she was hopeless in negotiations of this sort.

This was especially true when she thought that not only did the pots of cream not cost them anything like ten shillings to make, but it was in fact embarrassing to be in the position of having to sell anything.

It meant so much to Penelope that, despite her conscience, which pricked her all the time, they were spending the money which came from the Earl. Alisa tried to be happy about it.

When they finally got down to choosing their gowns, it was a thrill she had never enjoyed before to know how different she could look dressed in the height of fashion.

It was Penelope, of course, who contrived to make Mrs. Lulworth interested in them as social assets, by saying:

"We are staying with our aunt, Lady Ledbury, in Islington, and it is very important that my sister and I should have something fashionable to wear before we call on a very old friend of my mother's, the Marchioness of Conyngham."

Alisa thought that Mrs. Lulworth looked startled before she asked:

"Did you say—the Marchioness of Conyngham?"

"Yes, that is right. My mother used to visit the Marchioness's family when she was a girl, and my sister and I intend to get in touch with her as soon as we have something respectable to wear."

"That is certainly something I did not expect," Mrs. Lulworth said almost beneath her breath, and Alisa wondered why she should be so astonished.

"Her Ladyship," Mrs. Lulworth went on, "has bought some gowns from me in the past, and I should very much like to have the privilege of dressing her again."

"Then you must certainly make us gowns which she will admire when we call on her," Penelope said.

With her usual quickness, she realised that Mrs. Lulworth was extremely impressed by the Marchioness of Conyngham, and she went on:

"I am not being conceited, Mrs. Lulworth, but I do know that my sister and I will 'pay with dressing,' as the saying goes."

Mrs. Lulworth realised that she must supply them with gowns immediately, and she produced some that were already half-finished.

As Penelope and Alisa looked so lovely in them, she said she would finish them off, then start making others for the lady who had originally ordered them.

Mrs. Lulworth's assistants were sent running from one end of the shop to the other to produce materials which were so beautiful that Alisa knew they would be very expensive.

The moment she was able to do so, she whispered in Penelope's ear:

"Please, please . . . we cannot afford to . . . spend so . . . much."

"Leave everything to me," Penelope replied, undoing a roll of blue silk the exact colour of Alisa's eyes and holding it up against her.

"Look!" she exclaimed, and she did not have to put into words how lovely Alisa would look in it.

When finally they left the shop it was already luncheon-time and they knew their aunt would be annoyed with them for being late.

But nothing mattered except that Mrs. Lulworth had promised that by the next morning she would deliver two day-gowns to 43 Islington Square, and two evening-gowns would be ready by tomorrow night if they had a fitting during the afternoon.

Alisa had the uncomfortable impression that Penelope had ordered a number of other gowns as well.

She was quite certain that the fifty pounds that had come from the Earl and the twenty-two pounds for the new pots of cream would not cover the cost of the gowns, bonnets, gloves, shoes, stockings, and sunshades which Penelope had stipulated as being absolutely essential.

She tried to say as much as they hurried back to Islington, but they were walking so quickly that conversation was impossible, and they were in fact both breathless by the time they reached their aunt's house.

To put Aunt Harriet in a good mood after luncheon, which had been delayed for over half-an-hour, Alisa repaired one of the hymn-books while Penelope sewed up the seams of a grey gown in a cheap and ugly cotton for some poor unfortunate black child who would undoubtedly look hideous in it.

"I have a treat for you tomorrow," Lady Ledbury

said when she came into the room where they were working.

"What is that, Aunt Harriet?" Alisa asked.

"I am going to take you to St. Mary's to hear the Choir practise for the Coronation Service. We are very proud that our boys have been chosen to augment the Choir at Westminster Abbey, and I know you will enjoy hearing them."

"I am sorry, Aunt Harriet," Penelope said quickly, before Alisa could speak, "but tomorrow afternoon we have planned to call on the Marchioness of Conyngham."

There was silence while her aunt stared at her in sheer astonishment.

"Did you say the Marchioness of Conyngham?" she asked.

"Yes, Aunt," Penelope answered. "As I expect you know, she was a close friend of Mama's, and we have something to take her which we are sure she will be very pleased to have."

"I do not believe it!" Lady Ledbury said. "I have never heard of your mother associating with the Marchioness!"

"She was not the Marchioness when Mama was young," Penelope explained. "She was Elizabeth Denison, and Mama used to stay with them. But of course after she was married she lived in the country, so it was difficult for them to meet."

"I cannot credit that what you are telling me is true," Lady Ledbury said, "and I do not believe that at this present moment the Marchioness is somebody with whom you should be closely acquainted."

Penelope looked at her aunt in surprise.

"What do you mean by that, Aunt Harriet?"

There was silence. Then Lady Ledbury said:

"I do not intend to elaborate on this matter or discuss it with anybody as young as yourselves, but I

think I should really prevent you from doing as you
intend."

"I cannot understand what you are saying," Penelope said. "If there is something against the Marchioness, then it would be wiser for you to tell us what
it is."

"It is something I cannot discuss with two young and
innocent girls," Lady Ledbury replied.

As she spoke, she rose and walked with dignity from
the room, while Penelope and Alisa stared at each other
in astonishment.

"What can this be about?" Penelope asked.

"Perhaps we ought to obey her and not take the . . .
letter to the . . . Marchioness,"Alisa said nervously.

"Do not be ridiculous!" Penelope answered. "If Aunt
Harriet disapproves of her, it means she will be charming and just the sort of person to help us."

She saw that her sister looked worried, and put out
her hand towards her.

"Stop making difficulties, Alisa," she said, "or when
you grow old you will look exactly like Aunt Harriet!"

It sounded so ridiculous that Alisa began to laugh.

"I would do anything rather than that!"

"So would I," Penelope agreed, "and it makes me
more determined than ever to call on the Marchioness."

* * *

Later that evening, Alisa had gone up to her bedroom and was wondering what was keeping Penelope
downstairs. Then her sister burst into the room.

She shut the door behind her and said:

"Alisa, what do you think? You will never believe it!
I have found out why Aunt Harriet disapproves of the
Marchioness of Conyngham!"

Alisa, who was half-undressed, sat down on her bed.

"What has she done?" she asked.

"Hold your breath and listen!" Penelope replied.

Then slowly and dramatically she declared:

"The Marchioness is the new favourite of the King!"

Chapter Four

The Marchioness of Conyngham was fat, religious, kindly, rich, and rapacious.

At fifty-two, with four grown-up children, she could hardly believe that her new Beau should be the King of England.

After twenty-seven years of marriage her beauty was beginning to fade, and although she had been greatly admired, nobody had ever said she was particularly amusing or outstandingly intelligent.

However, she was more shrewd than most people gave her credit for, and the King adored her.

For some time now he had been seeing less and less of Lady Hertford, who was tearful and angry at losing the Monarch's attention and was exceedingly spiteful to all her friends about the Marchioness.

The one thing that Elizabeth Conyngham really enjoyed was jewellery. She was excessively fond of clothes and money, but jewellery was something which brought a sparkle to her eyes and made her effusively grateful.

The King had realised this, and he was incessantly heaping presents of diamonds, pearls, and sapphires on her.

Those in attendance on His Majesty had always been aware that, for some unexplained reason, he had all his life needed a motherly and affectionate woman to fuss over and fondle, and he had invariably been in love with women older than himself.

The Marchioness was in fact five years younger than he, but there was no doubt that by her contemporaries she was counted amongst the Dowagers, and the *Beau Mond* was laughing heartily at the remark made by Lady Hertford's grandson, Lord Beauchamp, who seeing the King riding with the Marchioness in the Park, had exclaimed:

"My God! Grandmother must learn to ride, or it is all over with us!"

The King found with the Marchioness something that the other women with whom he had been enamoured had been unable to give him, and that was a family.

He loved the Conyngham children deeply, and he wrote to the Marchioness's youngest granddaughter, Maria, the most affectionate and touching letters.

At first people were incredulous at this new amatory obsession displayed by the King, then they were amused by it.

The King was so much in love that he even went on a strict diet to try to make himself more attractive, and ways of pleasing the Marchioness were in his thoughts both day and night.

However, quite a number of people were scandalised and shocked by the association, including the Marchioness's brother and Alisa.

At first she scornfully dismissed the information brought to her by Penelope as being merely belowstairs gossip.

"How can you discuss such things with the servants, Penelope?" she asked. "You know Mama would not approve."

"They are the only human beings in this gloomy house!" Penelope retorted. "In fact, I asked Martha very tactfully why Aunt Harriet was so disapproving of somebody who sounded so respectable."

Martha was their aunt's lady's-maid, housekeeper, and, because she usually had nobody else to talk to, confidante.

Martha had been with Lady Ledbury for thirty years, and although she was somewhat strait-laced and definitely Puritanical, Alisa liked her.

She had certainly been kind to them when they were younger and were sent early to bed with the sort of supper which Aunt Harriet considered good for children.

It was Martha who had brought them up jellies or grapes and sometimes a chocolate or two.

"Martha says," Penelope went on, "that the Marchioness of Conyngham is as fat as the King, and the Cartoonists are drawing scandalous pictures of them both. We must certainly look at them when we have the chance."

"Perhaps we had . . . better not . . . call on the . . . Marchioness," Alisa said in a hesitating voice.

"Not call on her?" Penelope exclaimed. "How can you be so foolish?"

"But if she is . . . improper . . ."

"If she has the King in her pocket, as Martha says she has," Penelope answered, "can you not see how advantageous it would be if she would ask us to only one party? We would meet everybody there—but everybody!"

It flashed through Alisa's mind that this could include the Earl, and she said quickly, without thinking:

"Please, Penelope . . . do not . . . insist on our taking her a . . . present and . . . trying to make her . . . help us."

"If you are going to be so stupid as to behave like Aunt Harriet," Penelope exclaimed, "then I will go and see the Marchioness alone!"

This was something which Alisa knew she could not allow her sister to do.

At the same time, she hoped fervently that what they had been told was untrue and that Martha had exaggerated what was being said.

After all, surely the Marchioness was too old for a flirtation with the King or anybody else, and perhaps it was only jealousy which made people say unkind things of a lady he wanted merely as a friend.

She prayed that this was the truth, but when they were going for their fittings at Mrs. Lulworth's the following afternoon, Penelope insisted on stopping outside the shop in Bond Street that sold the latest cartoons.

There in the window was one by Rowlandson depicting the King and the Marchioness, both looking grossly fat and extremely flirtatious.

Because Alisa felt it was degrading even to look at it, she took only one glance and then walked on, regardless of the fact that she was leaving Penelope behind her.

Only when her sister caught up with her did she say:

"I think it is . . . wrong for you to be . . . interested in such . . . things! And because you are young and a débutante, I do beg of you, if anybody . . . mentions, which I am sure they will not . . . the King's . . . association with the Marchioness, you will pretend you know . . . nothing about . . . it."

"Very well, Miss Prude," Penelope replied.

She would have said more, but she was determined to have her own way in calling on the Marchioness later in the afternoon, and she was afraid that if Alisa was too shocked she would definitely refuse to go with her.

The evening-gowns were so lovely that Penelope was in raptures over hers, and Alisa found it difficult to argue about the behaviour of two elderly strangers —which was really how she thought of them—when they had so much for which to be grateful.

Nor did she wish to think of the man to whom they

owed their gratitude! But there was no doubt that it was an exhilaration she had never known before, to realise that both she and Penelope could look so completely different and indeed so lovely in the gowns which made them as ethereal and graceful as any Greek goddess.

'We should wear these standing in one of the alcoves in the Earl's Dining-Room,' Alisa thought involuntarily, then rebuked herself for thinking of him again.

Mrs. Lulworth promised that the gowns would be delivered the next day, then added:

"You do me great credit, and I hope that if anybody asks you from where you purchased your gowns, you will give them my name."

"You know we will do that," Penelope answered.

"We are very, very grateful to you," Alisa added. "You have been very kind."

Mrs. Lulworth smiled, which was a rare occurrence.

"I've sold ten pots of face-creams already this morning," she said, "and I've only twenty-nine left."

"That is splendid!" Penelope cried. "Sometime next week my sister and I will have to go back to the country to make some more."

"We'd better wait and see," Mrs. Lulworth said cautiously, "but they may quite likely be needed."

As they walked from Bond Street towards the Marchioness's house, Alisa found herself once again trying to think that Martha's story of the King's love for their mother's old friend was merely gossip.

She could not imagine that anybody of her mother's generation would indulge in love-affairs, even with a King, and although she admitted that she was very ignorant about such matters, she supposed that people in love would kiss each other in the same way that the Earl had kissed her.

But it was not love he was offering her!

At the same time, she realised how little she understood what a man felt for a woman or a woman for a man, and it was something she had no wish to discuss with Penelope.

'If Mama were alive,' she thought, 'I would ask her.'

Then she admitted to herself that she could not have told even her mother that she had been kissed, nor could she have described the strange feeling it had aroused in her.

They neared the very impressive mansion which Penelope had learnt again from Martha, was where the Marchioness of Conyngham resided with those of her children who were unmarried.

"I am praying, Alisa," she said in a low voice, "and I hope you are too, that the Marchioness will be at home."

Alisa felt that if the truth were told she was praying the opposite, so that they could just leave their letter and go away. But she was aware that most Ladies of Fashion entertained their friends on one particular day of the week, the most usual choice being Wednesday or Thursday.

This was Wednesday, and, as if once again luck was on Penelope's side, the two girls saw that there were a number of smart and expensive-looking carriages standing outside the house, which made it obvious that this was in fact the day when the Marchioness was "At Home."

Penelope, with a self-confidence that Alisa admired and felt should be hers rather than her younger sister's, said to the Butler:

"Is Her Ladyship at home?"

"Yes, Madam. Her Ladyship is receiving," the Butler replied.

"Then would you be kind enough to give Her Ladyship this note," Penelope enquired, "and ask her if she will allow Miss Alisa and Miss Penelope Wynton to call on her?"

The Butler took the note and sent a footman hurrying up the double staircase to the landing from which came the sound of voices.

As they waited in the Hall, a carriage drew up outside, and two ladies dressed exceedingly elegantly with exquisite high bonnets trimmed with ostrich-feathers and gowns in the new shape, entered the house and proceeded up the stairs.

Penelope watched them, then said to Alisa in a low voice:

"They are smart, but not nearly as smart or as beautiful as we are! Stop looking so frightened, dearest! This is the moment we have been waiting for, and I promise you will not be disappointed."

Alisa tried to smile in response.

At the same time, she was wishing she were back at home in her shabby gown, looking at the daffodils in the Park and making face-creams in the Still-Room from her mother's recipes.

Then, looking at her sister, she thought it would be impossible for anybody to be as beautiful as Penelope.

Mrs. Lulworth had been very insistent that their gowns should, while being distinctive, complement each other's with the whole ensemble in each case being of one colour.

"*Madame* Vestris," she chatted as they were being fitted, "has always said that a Leading Lady should stand out and that the eyes of those applauding her should not be distracted by a multitude of bits and pieces, and that applies particularly to colour."

Alisa thought of the red coat *Madame* Vestris had worn and remembered that her hat was also red, as were her short boots.

The only exception had been her white breeches, but that was something which certainly need not concern Penelope or herself.

Penelope's gown was pink, the colour, Alisa thought

with a faint smile, of a rose. Her bonnet was trimmed
with roses and satin ribbons of the same colour, and
even her slippers, showing beneath the elaborately
decorated hem of her skirt, were pink.

It said much for Mrs. Lulworth's skill that neither the
colour nor the shape looked theatrical, while at the
same time it would be impossible for Penelope to
remain unnoticed.

With Alisa beside her, no-one with eyes in their head
could fail to stare at the two girls.

Alisa was dressed in very pale blue, the colour of a
spring sky, and her eyes, in contrast to her dazzlingly
white skin, appeared to hold mysterious depths in
them.

Mrs. Lulworth had trimmed her bonnet with forget-
me-nots and there was a small border of blue veiling
round the edge of the brim.

"You look as if you had stepped out of the mists in the
early morning!" Penelope had remarked when she was
dressed.

"You are being poetical," Alisa said with a smile, and
instantly thought of the books of poetry in the Earl's
Library.

The footman came hurrying down the stairs and both
girls held their breath. He spoke to the Butler, and
Alisa thought with a little throb of apprehension how
disappointed Penelope would be if they were turned
away.

The Butler moved towards them and spoke to Penelope.

"Her Ladyship will be delighted to receive you,
Miss," he said in a courteous tone, then went up the
stairs in front of them.

As they entered the large Drawing-Room, which
covered the whole width of the house at the back and
looked over the garden, Alisa felt that everything swam

in front of her eyes and she could see nothing but a sea of faces.

However, there were not many people there, as she could see when her vision cleared, and it was not difficult to pick out the Marchioness, who looked exactly the way she had been portrayed in the cartoon.

"Miss Alisa and Miss Penelope Wynton, M'Lady!" the Butler boomed, and a large, Junoesque figure advanced towards them with outstretched hands.

"My dears! How delightful to meet you!" the Marchioness exclaimed. "I have often thought of your dear mother, and I an deeply grieved to hear that she is no longer with you."

Alisa curtseyed, then looked up into the Marchioness's face to see that there was a smile on her lips and she did in fact look kind and sincerely pleased to see them.

Alisa felt she would have known at once if what she was saying was merely polite, and the Marchioness continued:

"There is a distinct resemblance to your mother in both of you, and how very pretty you both are! I am sure you will have a most successful time now that you have come to London. Is your father here with you?"

"No, Ma'am, he is in Scotland," Penelope replied.

"He sent us to London to stay with his sister, Lady Ledbury, but it is very, very dull there and we did so hope you would remember Mama and be kind to us."

Alisa drew in her breath.

She had never imagined for one moment that Penelope would be so outspoken or make a plea for help immediately on meeting the Marchioness.

But a moment later she realised that Penelope, as usual, had been quick-witted enough to take advantage of an opportunity which might never come again,

While the Marchioness was talking to them no-one else happened to be trying to attract her attention, so, as Penelope would have said herself in the colloquial manner which Alisa always deplored, she was "striking while the iron was hot!"

"That, my dears," the Marchioness exclaimed, "is something I am certainly ready to do!"

"Mama always told us how kind you were to her when she was a girl," Penelope went on, "and that is why my sister Alisa and I have brought you something which belonged to Mama, and which we hoped you would like to have."

"How very sweet of you!" the Marchioness purred.

Alisa produced the present she was carrying, which they had wrapped in the soft paper in which their gowns from Mrs. Lulworth had been packed, and had tied it up with a bow of blue ribbon.

It certainly looked an attractive gift as she handed it to the Marchioness.

"I am going to open this later, when I am not so busily engaged," she said, "and when we can talk about your dear mother and I can tell you how lovely she was and how fond we were of each other."

She smiled.

"But now I must introduce you to my friends. It happens we are having a small dinner-party here to-morrow night for my daughter Elizabeth. The young people will dance afterwards and you must certainly join us."

"Oh, thank you, Ma'am!" Penelope cried. "Alisa and I were so afraid we would never have the chance of dancing in London, and it is something I would love more than anything else."

"I will see that you have plenty of opportunities to dance and to meet some charming young men," the Marchioness promised.

Then she took them round the room to present them to the other callers.

They drove home in a hackney-carriage because

Penelope said she was too exhausted to walk and also because it was getting too late for it to be proper for them to be on the streets alone.

"I cannot believe that what is happening is true!" she exclaimed.

"You were right and I was wrong," Alisa admitted. "Her Ladyship is exactly the sort of friend Mama would have, and I do not believe one word of all the wicked things which have been said about her and the King."

"No, of course not."

Alisa thought there was a note in Penelope's voice which did not ring true, but for her sister's sake she was in fact too glad, at what had happened to make any comment.

It would have been impossible for either of them not to realise that the Marchioness's manner towards them had impressed all her visitors.

They were mostly friends of her own age, but a few had brought their husbands, who had looked, Alisa thought, at Penelope and herself in a way that she was quite certain would discourage their wives from inviting them to any parties they were giving.

However, two or three ladies did say that they would ask the Marchioness for their address and promised to invite them to parties later in the Season, and it was only the younger women, Alisa thought, whose eyes had been undisguisedly hostile and who had obviously no wish to further an acquaintance with two undoubted potential rivals.

The mere fact that they were to dine at the Marchioness's house on Thursday night was to send Penelope into a transport of delight, about which she talked all the way home.

"We are launched, Alisa! Do you realise it? We are launched on the social scene! It is the most exciting thing that has ever happened to us."

"It is all due to you, dearest," Alisa replied "and I

can only hope that our frail little boats will not sink."

"Why should they?" Penelope asked. "And we shall need more than one gown each."

"Oh, no!" Alisa cried. "We cannot afford any more!"

"With Mrs. Lulworth already asking for more pots? You really are chicken-hearted, Alisa! Besides, supposing we do get into difficulties, we can pay our bills the moment we are married."

"Do not go so fast, Penelope! We have only been invitied to one dance, and already you are talking of being married, and doubtless to a Duke!"

"I was thinking of not less than a Prince!" Penelope retorted.

They both laughed so much that it was impossible to continue the conversation.

* * *

Walking in the garden at the back of the Marchioness's house, which was lit with Chinese lanterns hanging from the trees and tiny lights edging the paths, Alisa felt she had stepped into a dream.

It was difficult enough to believe that Penelope's outrageous plan of launching them into Society would succeed, without finding that there really was a distinct similarity between their story and that of the Gunning Sisters.

Certainly the invitation-card that had been delivered at Islington Square from the Marchioness the following morning surprised Lady Ledbury.

Strangely, it silenced any protests she might have made about accepting it, and the same morning there had been two other invitations from hostesses to whom they could not remember being introduced by the Marchioness and who may just have heard about them.

"Once we are talked about," Penelope said, "everybody will want us."

"How do you know such things, dearest?" Alisa
enquired.

"I am still remembering the story of the Gunning
Sisters. The moment people began to talk about them,
they were asked everywhere. Hostesses always like to
have the latest lion in tow."

"Is that what we are now?" Alisa enquired.

"I hope so," Penelope said fervently, but even she
was a little apprehensive on their way to the dinner-
party.

"This is the really crucial test," she said.

"Of what?"

"As to whether we are a sensation or not. After all, so
far we have not been up agianst any competition, but
tonight there will not only be girls of our own age but
the fascinating, sophisticated beauties who are pursued
relentlessly by the Bucks of St. James's, while their
husbands are pursuing somebody else's wife."

Alisa stiffened.

"That is not the sort of thing, Penelope, that you
should say?"

"I am only saying it to you," her sister answered.
"If you will not listen, I shall have to find somebody
else to talk to."

She was only teasing, but Alisa thought that one safe-
guard in respect to Penelope's impetuosity was that
they talked frankly with each other, and she hoped,
although she was not sure, that she curbed her sister's
tendency to act without thinking.

She did not like to think of Penelope knowing and
inevitably talking about the improprieties committed by
the King or anybody else.

Yet she knew that it was impossible to stop people
from gossiping about such things, and whatever she
might or might not say, excesses certainly did take
place.

Then inevitably she thought of her own behaviour, and shied away from the memory of the Earl like a young horse frightened by a leaf blowing across the road.

The Marchioness's impressive house looked very attractive at night, with the flaming torches which the linkmen had already lit, the red carpet laid outside the door, and the carriages queueing up to drop off their occupants one by one.

Alisa felt that perhaps they had been rather rude in not ensuring that their aunt was included in the invitation, but she was not quite certain how she should go about it, even if she had wished for Lady Ledbury to accompany them.

When she had suggested to Penelope that it was impolite to leave her behind, her sister had exclaimed:

"For goodness' sake, Alisa, the last thing we want is Aunt Harriet looking like the skeleton at the feast, and doubtless handing the King a tract on immorality."

Alisa laughed because she could not help it. Then she said in a low voice:

"You do not think the . . . King will be . . . there?"

"No, of course not," Penelope replied.

But again there had been a note in her voice which had made Alisa feel apprehensive.

As they entered the front door there seemed to be a whole army of servants in smart gold-braided uniforms and wearing white breeches and powdered wigs.

Having taken off their wraps, which matched their gowns and which Alisa was quite sure was another costly extra which would have to be paid for sooner or later, they proceeded up the stairs.

The Marchioness, looking more Junoesque than ever, and glittering with diamonds so that she looked, Alisa thought, as if she were enveloped in the whole Milky Way, received them with a smile and kissed them on both cheeks.

"Welcome, welcome, my dears!" she said effusively, nodding her head, on which there was a large white feather secured by a hugh diamond brooch.

"These are Lady Wynton's daughters, my dear," she added to the Marquis who was receiving beside her, and when he had shaken them by the hand they were introduced to his daughter, for whom the dance was being given.

At dinner Alisa found herself seated next to a middle-aged man who paid her several compliments. Then, finding that she came from the country and was interested in horses, he embarked on a long, rather uninteresting discourse on the merits and successes of various racing-stables.

On her other side was a vacant-looking man who, from his appearance, she guessed to be a Dandy. His cravat was so high and so tight that he obviously found it difficult to eat and to talk.

She did her best, but she found him a bore and turned back to her racing-friend with relief.

She discovered that he was a widower and the father of a débutante who was, like Penelope, just seventeen, and this was only the second party to which she had been invited in London.

When she met the girl when dinner was over, Alisa felt sorry for her. She was obviously extremely shy, and, with few pretensions to good looks, she would in fact have made a far more handsome horse!

When dinner was finished and the ladies retired to leave the gentlemen to their port, they were with few exceptions very polite to Alisa and Penelope.

Then other guests began to arrive and Alisa found that far from being a small party, as the Marchioness had described it, it appeared to be quite a large one.

Downstairs there was a Ball-Room decorated with wreaths of flowers, its windows opening onto the garden, and a Band whose music transported her into a dream world which she thought existed only in books.

The gentlemen whom they had met at dinner seemed only too eager to dance with her and Penelope, and she knew by the expression on her sister's face how happy she was.

The garden was like a fairy land, Alisa thought, as she walked in it with her partner, who was the older gentleman who had sat next to her at dinner.

But she knew she must not go far from the lights of the house or be inveigled into sitting in the arbours which she could see arranged in the shadows amongst the flowering shrubs.

"I should have warned Penelope to be on her guard," Alisa told herself.

She could not help thinking that if the Earl had been prepared to kiss her in the Library after luncheon, to be alone with a man with stars in the sky above them and music playing softly in the distance was an invitation to indiscretion.

"I hope one day, Miss Wynton," her partner was saying, "you will come and see some of my race-horses that I keep at Epson. I am sure you would appreciate that they are outstanding."

"I am certain you are very successful," Alisa said with a smile.

"I hope to be even more so," he answered, "and especially to win the Gold Cup at Ascot this year."

"Which of your horses are you entering?" Alisa asked. "If you will tell me his name, I will send up a very special prayer that he will win."

"It is very properly named *Victorious*, and because I am certain that we shall meet a great deal before Ascot, I shall keep you to your promise."

"My father has told me that the Gold Cup at Ascot is one of the most coveted prizes that every owner longs to win," Alisa said.

"That is true enough," her companion replied, "but

Victorious will have to beat a very outstanding horse which has unfortunately pipped him at the post at several race-meetings recently."

"And what is his name?" Alisa enquired.

"*Apollo*. I am sure you must have heard of him, because he belongs to the Earl of Keswick."

"The Earl of . . . Keswick?"

Alisa was not certain whether she had said the words aloud or in her mind.

"He has certainly been very lucky with *Apollo*, so you see, Miss Wynton, I shall certainly need your prayers."

As they were talking they had reached the end of the path lined with fairy-lights, and now they turned to walk back towards the house.

It was then, as they did so, that the owner of *Victorious* exclaimed:

"Talk of the Devil, as the saying goes—there is the Earl! I thought he would arrive with the King."

Alisa felt that it was impossible to breathe, for there, standing just inside the open windows of the Ball-Room, she could clearly see George IV, and beside him, tall and slim and equally resplendent, was the Earl of Keswick!.

For a moment she longed to run away, to hide, to escape.

It flashed through her mind that she should find Penelope and say she was ill.

Then she remembered that in that case she would be obliged to explain to her hostess why she wished to leave, and the Marchioness would be beside the King, with the Earl in attendance.

She felt as though everything was jumbled dizzily in her mind, and she could not sort out anything or make a decision.

And all the time she was walking towards the Ball-Room, while the gentleman beside her was talking.

"I hope you will dance with me again, Miss Wynton,"
he said. "In fact, when I have done my duty with two of
the ladies with whom we had dinner, I shall come and
look for you."

"Thank . . . you," Alisa managed to say, but her voice
did not sound like her own.

They stepped in through the window and as they did
so she told herself that it was very unlikely the Earl
would recognise her.

He had only seen her in the drab gown in which she
had had luncheon with him, and she was certain that
she looked entirely different in the beautiful, expensive
one she wore now and with her hair arranged in the
latest fashion.

"Besides," she asked herself, "why should he expect
to see me with the Marchioness of Conyngham?"

She stole a quick glance at him and thought he was
looking bored and at the same time awe-inspiring, as he
had when she had first looked at him in *Madame*
Vestris's dressing-room.

Then she turned her face away so that if he did
glance in her direction, all he would see would be the
back of her head, and, still escorted by her racing-
friend, she proceeded to the far end of the Ball-Room,
where to her relief she caught sight of Penelope.

Her sister was talking animatedly to a good-looking
young man who she noticed had been beside her at
dinner.

As Alisa joined them, the gentleman who had escorted
her bowed and moved away, and Penelope said:

"Oh, dearest, I want you to meet Major James Coombe.
He is going to ask us both to the Trooping of the
Colour, which he tells me is a brilliant spectacle!"

"Almost as spectacular as you and your sister, Miss
Wynton," the Major said gallantly.

Penelope laughed.

Introducing the Romantic World of Barbara Cartland Fragrances

A world of rare and exotic perfumes…
Inspired by the intensely romantic raptures
of love in every Barbara Cartland novel.

Experience the World of Barbara Cartland Fragrances

Awaken the romantic in your soul. With the mysteriously beautiful perfumes of romance inspired by Barbara Cartland. There's a heady floral bouquet called *The Heart Triumphant,* an exotic Oriental essence named *Moments of Love* and *Love Wins,* a tantalizing woodsy floral. Each of the three, blended with the poetry and promise of love. For every woman who has ever yearned to love. Yesterday, today and especially tomorrow!

Available at fragrance counters everywhere.

Helena Rubinstein®

"That is the sort of flattering thing he says, but I do not believe a word of it!"

"Now that is very unkind!" the Major expostulated. "I can swear that everything I have said to you tonight is completely true and would come from the very depths of my heart if I had one."

Alisa laughed, but she was sure he was completely bowled over by Penelope's loveliness, and she was not surprised.

She could not imagine that anybody could look more fascinating than her sister did at this moment.

Her eyes were shining like the stars overhead because she was so happy and excited.

The next dance was starting and now half-a-dozen young men rushed up to claim a dance either with Penelope or with Alisa.

Those who were disappointed said:

"Please promise me the next, promise! Promise!"

Alisa had been told by her mother that Balls were usually very formal and no gentleman would ask a girl to dance unless he was introduced to her by a hostess or a lady acting in that capacity.

Now she understood that this was an informal party and why the Marchioness had referred to it as being "little."

It was certainly much more fun, but now as her partner danced with her to the end of the room she saw the Earl.

He was still standing near the King, who was seated on a sofa, holding the Marchioness's hand in his and whispering in her ear in a very intimate manner.

There was no doubt, Alisa thought, that the Earl was looking even more bored than he had been when they had first arrived, and she thought too there was a frown between his eyes.

She turned her head away as they passed him, but

she had the feeling that his thoughts were far away, and she wondered if perhaps *Madame* Vestris had been difficult or if he might be cross that he could not be with her tonight, taking her to supper after the Show.

She wondered where they would go and what they would talk about and if the conversation would be as interesting as she had found it when she and the Earl had had luncheon together.

She imagined them having supper, perhaps by candlelight, perhaps at *Madame*'s house or at his, and she wondered if he would kiss her in the Library as he had kissed her.

With a start, Alisa realised that the dance had come to an end and her partner was waiting for an answer to a question she had not heard.

"I am sorry . . . I did not hear what you . . . said," she explained.

As she spoke, she saw that the Earl had moved from where he had been standing and was only a few feet away from her.

Then as she looked into his eyes she saw a surprised look of recognition in his.

"I asked you if you would dine with my mother tomorrow night. She is giving a party for my sister," her partner was saying, "and I could arrange for you and your sister to be invited. Please tell me you will come."

"Thank you. Thank you . . . very much!" Alisa answered, hardly aware of what she was saying.

Then, as if she was compelled by some force over which she had no control, she moved away from him towards the Earl.

Only as she reached him did she know what she had to do, and it was imperative that she should do it at once.

She was too shy to look again at his face, fixing her eyes instead on his cravat, which vaguely at the back of her mind she thought was even more intricately tied than when she had first seen him, and she said:

"Please . . . could I . . . speak to . . . you?"

She could hardly hear her own voice, and yet he must have heard what she had said, for he replied:

"Of course. Shall we go into the garden?"

They walked down the room, Alisa taking two steps to his one, and she felt almost as if she were being taken to her execution.

It flashed through her mind that unless she could persuade him to do what she wanted, she and Penelope would have to refuse every invitation, and she knew that her sister would never forgive her.

The Earl walked not along the lighted path as Alisa had done before, but across to where under the trees and sheltered by the foliage there was an empty seat with cushions on it.

He waited for Alisa to sit down, then he sat beside her and, turning sideways, rested his arm across the back of the seat.

She was acutely conscious that his penetrating eyes were on her face and it was impossible to look at him.

She could only twist her fingers together in an effort to think wildly of what she should say.

Then at last, as he did not speak, she said:

"Please . . . forgive me . . . I know it was . . . wrong and you must be . . . angry . . . but we . . . kept the money because it . . . meant so much . . ."

What she said sounded inadequate and very hesitant, and the Earl said:

"You said you wanted to do something special, and I presume that meant buying the gown you are wearing now."

Alisa thought it was clever of him to guess the reason so quickly, and she answered:

"I wanted to . . . send the cheque back . . . but if I

had . . . done so, I think I would have . . . broken my sister's heart . . . She felt it was a . . . gift from the . . . gods."

There was a faint smile on the Earl's face as he said:

"The gods certainly look after their own, and when you ran away I had the idea that you might have fled back to Olympus."

She thought he was laughing at her, and she said:

"It may seem to . . . you that we . . . stole your money, but I . . . swear that I will . . . pay you back, even though it may . . . take a long . . . time."

"With the proceeds from your creams?"

"We have sold a lot of those already, and that is . . . another thing I . . . wanted to . . . speak to you . . . about."

As she spoke, she felt as if the words were almost strangled in her throat, and after a moment's silence, the Earl said:

"I am waiting."

"The Marchioness of Conyngham and my mother were friends when they were girls . . . and she asked us here . . . tonight, and we have had other . . . invitations as well . . ."

She looked up at the Earl pleadingly.

" . . . But please . . . please," she went on bravely, "I beg of you . . . not to tell . . . anybody that we sell . . . face-creams or that I . . . kept the money you . . . gave me."

"Do you imagine I might do that?" the Earl enquired.

Alisa made a helpless little gesture with her hands.

"If you do, you . . . know that we will be ostracised and . . . nobody will . . . speak to us."

"Which means, of course, that you would have to revert to working for the Missionaries."

"Yes . . . that is . . . true," Alisa said with something suspiciously like a sob. "It is what my aunt . . . expected us to do when we . . . arrived in London . . . but instead . . ."

Her voice died away.

"You spent my fifty pounds on your clothes!"

Alisa nodded. Then she said, still in the pleading voice she had used before:

"How could we go . . . anywhere or . . . meet any-body . . . dressed in the gowns we had made . . . ourselves, and which were out of . . . fashion? You saw how I . . . looked when we . . . met."

"In *Madame* Vestris's dressing-room," the Earl said. "Hardly the place for a débutante!"

"I know it was . . . wrong, but we thought the only way we could obtain a little . . . money was to sell the . . . herbal creams which Mama taught us how to make, and Mrs. Lulworth said that if *Madame* Vestris . . . liked the creams . . . everybody would want to buy them . . . and they are . . . selling!"

"You do not think that Mrs. Lulworth will betray you?"

"No, she has . . . promised on her . . . honour that she will tell . . . nobody where the creams come . . . from, and I am not . . . likely to see . . . *Madame* Vestris again . . . no-one else but . . . you saw me there."

"You did not think when you came to the Theatre you were likely to meet men there?"

"No . . . but now I am . . . afraid."

"Afraid?"

"That you may tell people, and also . . ."

There was silence.

"I would like to hear the end of that sentence," the Earl said.

The colour rose in Alisa's face, as she remembered how he had kissed her and what she had felt, and because she found it impossible to speak of such things she looked away from him across the garden.

"I suppose," the Earl said after what seemed a long silence, "you were shocked at what I suggested to you?"

"Very . . . shocked!"

"I can hardly blame you, but I did not realise that a seller of face-creams was a Lady of Quality!"

He was speaking in the dry, mocking tone she had heard so often before, and she answered impulsively:

"You are . . . laughing at me . . . and I know it was wrong . . . very wrong to have . . . luncheon with you . . . alone . . . but I was . . . hungry and I knew that Papa would not . . . wish me to eat . . . in a . . . public place."

"When did you realise it was wrong?" the Earl asked. "You did not appear to think so at the time."

"Penelope told me I should not have gone to a . . . gentleman's house, and I realised that was true . . . when it was . . . too late."

"Too late to prevent me from kissing you!"

Alisa dropped her head.

"I am . . . very . . . ashamed," she whispered.

"There is nothing for which you need be ashamed," the Earl said quietly. "And I thought, although I might have been mistaken, that while I am aware it was the first time you had been kissed, you did not find it repulsive."

"No . . . of course . . . not! It was just . . . something I . . . should not have . . . allowed."

"I think you could not have prevented it from happening."

Alisa knew this was true. Then he said quietly:

"If it upsets you, forget that it happened."

It flashed through her mind that that was impossible. At the same time, his words made her ask:

"Will you . . . forget that you have . . . ever met me . . . before this . . . moment?"

"Shall I say that I will not speak of it to anybody?"

"Do you . . . really mean that? Do you . . . promise?" Alisa asked.

As she spoke she looked eagerly up at the Earl, and now as her eyes met his she felt as if he held her spellbound and as if once again she was in his arms.

Almost as if she were swept back into the past, she felt that strange and rapturous feeling within her, rising from her breasts to her throat and from her throat to her lips.

It was so perfect that it was like the music she could hear in the distance and the soft rustle of the trees overhead, while for the moment it was impossible to look away or even to breathe.

"I have given you my word, Alisa," the Earl said, "so now enjoy yourself and believe that what the gods have given the gods will not take away."

As she opened her lips to thank him, he rose to his feet.

"Come," he said. "I will take you back to the Ball-Room. We must not have the gossips talking about you, as they will undoubtedly do if we stay here any longer."

The dry, cynical note was back in his voice, but as Alisa walked beside him towards the lights, her heart was singing.

Chapter Five

There was a loud rat-tat on the front door which echoed through the house, and Penelope looked at Alisa and smiled.

"More flowers?" she exclaimed.

The room certainly did not look as though it needed any more, and the two girls were overcome every day with the bouquets which kept arriving at their aunt's house and the invitations which poured in.

The servants had already complained that their feet were giving out from running up and down from the basement to answer the front door, and even Lady Ledbury was astonished at the commotion her nieces were causing.

What was more, the more traditional hostesses had included her in their invitations, and while at first Lady Ledbury wished to refuse, it was Alisa who persuaded her to attend one or two of the Assemblies and Receptions to which they were asked.

For the first time Lady Ledbury became feminine and exclaimed:

"How can I possibly go anywhere? I have no clothes for that sort of thing."

It was Alisa who persuaded her to buy a new gown and bonnet which were in blue rather than black, and when she had her hair arranged by the same hairdresser who attended the house almost daily for the two girls, she really looked rather handsome.

"Why do you bother with the old thing?" Penelope asked when she and Alisa were alone.

"I am sorry for her."

"She is quite happy with her Missionaries and her tracts."

"I think she was drawn to good works," Alisa said, "because she had nothing else."

Penelope looked at her sister in surprise as she went on:

"Can you imagine how empty her life must be when she has only those dreary Missionaries fussing all the time about black children being naked and the Vicar who can talk of nothing but raising money for his Church?"

Impulsively, Penelope kissed her sister.

"You always have something nice to say about everybody, dearest," she said. "Whoever you marry will be a very lucky man."

Penelope had already had one proposal of marriage, but it was from a rather stupid young man and she would not have thought of accepting him.

At the same time, it was encouraging, and now as the two girls hurried down the stairs to the Drawing-Room, they found, as they had expected, the old parlour-maid taking in a bouquet, a basket filled with orchids, and a long flower box.

"More flowers, Henderson!" Penelope remarked.

"As ye says, Miss," Henderson replied tartly, "an' I hopes it's the last! I'm too old to keep coming up and down them stairs!"

She set the basket of orchids down on the floor at Penelope's feet, then shuffled away as if her legs were too tired to carry her.

"Perhaps we could persuade Aunt Harriet to have a

young footman temporarily, now that we are here," Alisa said.

Penelope did not answer.

She was looking at the note which was attached to the basket of orchids, and when she saw there was a crest on it, she exclaimed with a note of triumph:

"It is from your Duke."

Alisa frowned.

"He is not *my* Duke."

"Of course he is!" Penelope replied. "And judging by the size of the basket and the expense of the orchids, it will not be long before he asks you to become his Duchess."

Alisa took the note which her sister held out to her and saw written on it the words:

> *"To thank you for two very enjoyable dances.*
> *Exminster.*

She had been surprised when she found that the gentleman she had sat next to at the dinner-party that first night at the Marchioness's house was the Duke of Exminster.

She had learnt that he was a widower and she knew from their conversation that he was a racing enthusiast.

It was Penelope who had learnt that he owned the best racing-stable in the country, and his only rival was the Earl of Keswick.

The Duke had attached himself to Alisa at every party since, and because she realised that he was growing more possessive in his attitude, she had last night deliberately danced with him only twice and managed to avoid a quiet *tête-a-tête* that he obviously wished to have with her.

It was difficult to explain to Penelope why she did not

want him to come to the point of proposing marriage, which she sensed instinctively was in his mind.

She knew only that the idea of marriage to somebody so much older than herself frightened her, and now that she was actually confronted with what had only been a fantasy, she wished to avoid committing herself in any way.

As she could not discuss her feelings for the Duke of Exminster with Penelope, she put down his note and said quickly:

"What flowers have you received, dearest?"

Penelope had in her hand the long flower-box. She opened it and inside Alisa could see that there was just one pink rose.

"What a strange gift!" she exclaimed. "Who sent you that?"

Her sister held out the card that was in the box and on it Alisa read:

From a rose to its twin.

She laughed.

"You can never get away from being described as a rose, dearest, and of course in your pink gown you look exactly like one."

"I am sick of being told so," Penelope said sharply, "and that tiresome Major Coombe keeps teasing me about it."

"It is really a compliment."

"It is one I do not want from him!"

She picked up the bouquet and said:

"This is better! I have the wonderful idea, dearest, that you and I will beat the Gunning Sisters."

"In what way?"

"You will marry a Duke and so shall I."

Alisa looked at Penelope wide-eyed.

"Do you mean the Duke you were dancing with last night?"

"Of course I do!" Penelope replied. "And I can assure you he is very ardent."

She watched the expression on Alisa's face as she went on:

"If we both become Duchesses, I am sure we will be in the history books."

Alisa was silent.

When she had been introduced to the Duke of Hawkeshead, she had thought him an extremely unprepossessing man.

He had a red face and was not in the least good-looking. Moreover, she had not liked the manner in which he was looking at Penelope, which somehow, although she could not explain it exactly, seemed an impertinence.

He had also been somewhat untidily dressed, and towards the end of the evening she had noticed that he got even redder in the face and talked over-loudly as if he had been drinking a great deal.

She wanted to say to Penelope that the Duke was the last sort of man she wanted her to marry.

Then she thought it would be a mistake to sound too critical, and she merely said:

"You are such a success, dearest, there is no hurry for you to make up your mind. I think Aunt Harriet is quite resigned to having us here. In fact, although she wouldn't admit it, she is enjoying the excitement of it all."

"Of course she is," Penelope agreed. "And that reminds me, I forgot to tell you there was a note last night from Mrs. Lulworth, saying that she wants some more creams immediately and is leaving two hundred empty pots here for us today."

"Two hundred!" Alisa exclaimed. "How splendid! Now perhaps we can afford one more gown each."

"I want a great deal more than that," Penelope answered. "I cannot bear to be seen again in pink, and my evening-gown is in tatters!"

Alisa knew this was almost true.

She and Penelope had both had to repair their gowns, and although they had tried to add different coloured ribbons, they were quite certain the women in the parties they attended were not deceived and knew that in fact they were each wearing the same gown night after night.

Alisa was mentally counting up how much money they would receive for two hundred pots, but they were already in debt to Mrs. Lulworth and she was very much against asking her for more credit.

She did not have to speak for Penelope to know what she was thinking.

"Oh, for Heaven's sake, Alisa!" she said. "Let us enjoy ourselves while we have the chance, and if both our future husbands are enormously rich, why should we have to pinch and scrape to please nothing but your tiresome conscience?"

"I wish you would not talk as if I had agreed to . . . marry the Duke, who has not even . . . asked me," Alisa said.

"But he intends to do so, and you will accept him, so why pretend?"

"I have not decided . . . whether I will or . . . not," Alisa replied in a small voice.

"How can you be so ridiculous?" Penelope asked. "Have you forgotten the alternative to being a Duchess? To go back to the country and sit, seeing nobody and doing nothing but copying out Papa's manuscripts."

"I had you, and I was very happy," Alisa said.

The way she spoke made Penelope immediately contrite.

"Forgive me, dearest, for being so horrid, but you know that what is happening now will never happen again."

She felt that Alisa did not understand, and she explained:

"We are a success because we are new and the *Beau Monde* is always intrigued by something new and sensational. But in a few months, perhaps sooner, they will be used to us. Then there will be other sisters, perhaps even triplets, to take our place, and we shall be forgotten."

Alisa laughed.

"I do not think that is likely to happen, but I understand what you are saying."

"We must be like the farmers at home," Penelope said, "who always say: 'Make hay while the sun shines,' and that is what we have to do. So thank your Duke very prettily for the flowers and promise to dance with him at my Duke's Ball the night after next."

"He is giving a Ball?" Alisa exclaimmed in surprise.

"He says it is for me," Penelope replied, "and I have the feeling that he intends to propose to me that evening, then announce it. He likes to cause a sensation."

It flashed through Alisa's mind that that was the last way in which she would wish to proclaim her engagement, for she was sure it would be very embarrassing. But again she thought it would be a mistake to say so, and instead she asked:

"When do you plan that we shall go to the country to make the face-creams?"

"I suppose we shall have to go tomorrow," Penelope answered. "The only invitation we shall have to chuck is with that boring friend of Aunt Harriet's who is giving a luncheon simply because we are fashionable."

"Perhaps it would be unkind to behave like that to her," Alisa suggested.

"I am not concerned with her feelings," Penelope replied, "but it is a terrible bore to have to waste a whole day by going home."

"There is no need for you to come," Alisa said. "I can catch an early Stage-Coach and I am sure there will be one returning late in the afternoon."

"I have a better idea!" Penelope exclaimed.

There was another rat-tat on the door and another bouquet of flowers, and Alisa forgot to ask Penelope what it was she had been about to say.

She learnt what her sister was planning late that evening after they had been to a very grand Reception at the French Embassy at which both the King and the Earl had been present.

Alisa had not spoken to the Earl alone, but she had been vividly aware that he was there and also that while she was talking to the Duke of Exminster his eyes were watching her.

She thought he looked more bored and cynical than usual, until she noticed him talking to a very attractive lady with dark hair and flashing eyes, who was not unlike *Madame* Vestris.

"I suppose he only admires brunettes," she told herself, and wondered why the thought was curiously depressing.

It was when they got home just before midnight that Penelope said:

"I have fixed everything for tomorrow."

"What do you mean?" Alisa enquired.

"We are going to the country with four horses, which means it will not only be quicker but far less tiring."

Alisa looked at her in surprise, and Penelope exclaimed:

"You can guess whose carriage will be taking us! After all, there is only one person to whom our cream-making is no secret."

"You cannot mean . . . the Earl?"

"Of course it is the Earl," Penelope replied. "When I told him tonight what we had to do, he said at once that his horses will be at our disposal."

"How could you do such a thing?" Alisa asked almost angrily. "We are under an . . . obligation to him already, and I have no desire to make it . . . worse!"

"You became involved with him in the first place," Penelope said, "and actually there was no need for me to plead with him. I merely said that we had to leave the Reception early because we would have such a tiring day tomorrow. And when he asked me why and I told him that our creams were in such demand that Mrs. Lulworth wanted more, he said at once that he would arrange for us to travel in comfort."

"I wish you had discussed it with me first," Alisa said. Penelope laughed.

"You would only have said 'no,' and I should have asked him anyway, so what was the point?"

When Penelope had left her and Alisa was alone, she thought of quite a number of arguments she might have put forward to show that they should not accept any more favours from the Earl.

Then she told herself that there was no use trying to prevent Penelope from doing anything she wished to do.

"He must . . . think we are very . . . forward," she told herself before she went to sleep.

* * *

The following morning, she was just putting on her bonnet when Penelope burst into her room.

"Who do you think is waiting for us downstairs?" she asked.

The way she spoke made Alisa's heart miss a beat, but Penelope did not wait for her to reply.

"The Earl is driving us himself," she said, "and as the horses are fresh, he says we are not to keep him waiting!"

She slipped out of the room before Alisa could say anything, so she merely picked up the small case in which she had packed her old gown and an apron and ran down the stairs.

Outside the front door, looking magnificent and wearing his top-hat at a slightly raffish angle, was the Earl.

He was driving a different Phaeton from the High-Perched one in which Alisa had travelled the first time she had met him.

This one was lower and drawn by a team of four perfectly matched jet-black stallions. As he had rightly said, they were fresh and difficult to hold.

The two girls got in beside him, and, having stowed away the box that contained the pots from Mrs. Lulworth, the coachman jumped up behind and they were off.

It was only as they drove out of the Square that Alisa realised that having stepped into the Phaeton first, she was sitting next to the Earl, with Penelope on her other side.

He was concentrating on his horses, and Alisa thought that, perhaps because he was doing something he enjoyed, he did not look so bored as he did at the evening parties.

In fact as he glanced at her there was a faint smile on his lips as he said:

"You look surprised to see me."

"I am more than surprised . . . I am . . . apologetic," Alisa answered. "I had no idea . . . that you would put yourself to the trouble of driving us . . . yourself."

"I thought you would travel quicker, and I am also interested to see where you live, after you were so secretive about it."

Alisa remembered how she had avoided his questions the first time when she had had luncheon with him, and she replied:

"I do not think . . . you will find it very . . . exciting."

As the horses were travelling very fast, it was not possible to have much conversation during the journey, which they achieved in record time.

When they turned in at the ill-kept moss-covered drive and had their first glimpse of the Manor House, Alisa felt that for the moment it looked smaller than it had ever done before.

At the same time, its weather-beaten bricks and gabled roofs were beautiful because it was home.

It was then that the Earl told them what he intended to do.

"I have a friend not far from here who possesses some horses I want to see," he said. "What I suggest is that you do your work and I will return to have a late luncheon with you, after which I hope we shall be able to return to London."

"A . . . late . . . luncheon?" Alisa faltered.

She was thinking that there would be nothing in the house to eat, except possibly some eggs from the chickens which were often very erratic in their laying.

The Earl smiled.

"I have taken the precaution," he said, "of bringing my luncheon and yours with us."

Alisa drew in her breath.

Somehow she felt it was an insult that he should provide his own food. But then she told herself that he was only being practical, and there was nothing she could do but accept gracefully.

"It . . . is very kind of . . . you to be so . . . considerate," she said.

As she spoke, she thought that he knew her feelings, because there was a twinkle she disliked in his eyes and a distinct twist to his lips.

As soon as they were in the house and the Brigstocks had exclaimed with excitement at seeing them, Alisa and Penelope rushed upstairs to change their gowns for the old muslins they had made themselves, then hurried to the Still-Room.

Fortunately, Emily was there, and they sent her into the garden to pick the cucumbers and the lettuce-leaves, while Alisa started mixing the preparations which her mother had left behind her, and Penelope fetched the pots of honey they required.

They worked at a feverish pace.

Alisa was frightened that they would not have finished by the time the Earl returned and he would resent not being able to leave for London as soon as he wished to do.

Gradually, one by one, the pots were filled, and there were only eleven left empty for which they had not enough ingredients.

"They will have to wait for another day," Penelope said firmly. "Mrs. Lulworth is certain to want the strawberry-cream, but when I looked in the garden just now I saw it will be at least three weeks before they are ready."

"I hope we will have to come back to make more cream before that," Alisa replied.

"Actually, I feel in my bones that this will be the last batch we will ever make," Penelope said. "When we are Duchesses we will sweep into Mrs. Lulworth's shop and complain if she does not have a new and different sort of face-cream to offer us!"

Alisa laughed at the idea.

Yet, every time Penelope spoke about their being Duchesses, she had a strange sensation that was almost like a feeling of repugnance.

However, there was no time to think now, and when finally the pots were ready and she had changed her gown again and hurried downstairs, it was to find the Earl in their Sitting-Room, looking at her unfinished painting of the primroses.

"I am ... sorry if we have ... kept you ... waiting," Alisa said breathlessly.

"I was thinking that this would make an excellent pair to the one you have already given me," he replied.

It was the first time he had mentioned the painting she had sent him, and she blushed as she said:

"I thought . . . perhaps you would think it very poor . . . recompence for the very large . . . cheque you gave me . . . but there was . . . nothing in the house which would not look . . . ridiculous beside your . . . treasures."

"I was delighted to have it."

Alisa looked at him, wondering if he was speaking politely or if he meant what he said.

Then Penelope came into the room, crying:

"How could you have brought us such delicious things to eat? Mrs. Brigstock has set them all out in the Dining-Room, and I am so hungry that I cannot wait another moment!"

The Earl had certainly been very considerate, and as they sat down at the table where they had eaten for so many years, Alisa thought that because it was a picnic without servants to wait on them, it was the most enjoyable luncheon they had ever had.

Penelope chattered away, and the Earl, sitting between them in her father's chair, seemed relaxed and amused.

He had taken the precaution of bringing with him his own wines, and the only thing Mrs. Brigstock had to prepare was some hot coffee to end the meal.

"I could not eat another crumb!" Penelope exclaimed at length. "But I deserved every mouthful because Alisa and I have worked this morning at such a speed it would create a record anywhere in the world!"

"I am sure the women who benefit from your labours will appreciate it," the Earl said drily.

"The creams really are good!" Alisa said defiantly.

"I am aware of that," the Earl replied.

She thought he must have seen their beneficial effect on *Madame* Vestris, and she had a feeling that was almost one of pain, which she could not explain to herself.

"I think perhaps . . . you will want to be . . . returning to . . . London," she said.

She thought he might be planning to see *Madame* Vestris at the King's Theatre before her performance, or perhaps he was counting the hours until he could take her out to supper afterwards.

"There is no hurry," the Earl replied, "and Ben has to clear up what is left of our picnic, so I suggest you show me the rest of the house, which incidentally I find very attractive."

"You cannot mean . . . that!" Alisa exclaimed.

"Why not?" the Earl questioned. "Your home is Elizabethan, and it is a period which has always fascinated me."

Alisa's eyes widened.

"As it has me! I love to read about the way Queen Elizabeth lifted the heart of the nation and made us a great country."

"That is exactly what she did," the Earl agreed, "and we need another Queen to do the same thing today."

Alisa looked at him in surprise.

Then she remembered that since the death of Princess Charlotte, the heir to the throne, after the King's brothers who had no sons, would be the little daughter of the Duke of Kent, who was called Victoria.

"I think the Monarch should always be a man," Penelope said, "and the King I would like to have met is Charles II."

"Since he had an eye for a pretty woman, he would certainly have looked at you," the Earl said.

"Why not?" Penelope replied. "In which case I would have become a Duchess in my own right."

The Earl laughed.

"Is that what you are aiming for?"

"Of course!" Penelope replied. "You must have realised by now that Alisa and I are the Gunning Sisters up-to-date, and Elizabeth, the younger one, married two Dukes!"

The Earl lifted his glass and said with a twinkle in his eyes:

"May you succeed in your ambitions."

As he spoke, Alisa suddenly remembered that Maria, the elder sister, had married an Earl.

Quickly she pushed back her chair and rose from the table.

"If you will . . . excuse me," she said, "I have a . . . great many things to . . . see to . . . before we go back to . . . London."

Without looking at the Earl, she hurried from the room.

* * *

When they arrived home that evening, Penelope said:

"I must say, Alisa, the Earl was extremely helpful and far nicer than I thought he would be."

"He was very kind," Alisa murmured.

"It is a pity he is not a suitor for your hand," Penelope went on.

Her sister did not reply and she added:

"Major Coombe was telling me that the betting in White's Club is thirty-to-one against anybody catching the Earl as a husband."

"Why is he so . . . determined to remain . . . unmarried?" Alisa asked.

"Apparently he had an unfortunate love-affair when he was very young, and it made him swear that he would remain a bachelor in spite of the fact that his family have been on their knees for years begging him to produce an heir."

"I expect he has . . . plenty of . . . women in his . . . life," Alisa murmured, thinking of *Madame* Vestris.

"Of course there are hundreds of lovely ladies pursuing him!" Penelope agreed. "Major Coombe says they flutter round him like bees round a honey-pot, but the only things he is married to are his horses and his Estate in the country. Has he told you about his house?"

"No."

"It is said to be the most perfect example of Elizabethan architecture in England. That is why he was saying how much he admired Queen Elizabeth."

"I . . . did not . . . know."

"You are so stupid, Alisa!" Penelope complained. "You should ask people about their possessions. You know all men like to talk about themselves, and do not forget your Duke is interested in horses."

Alisa thought she was well aware of that and that she knew so much about the Duke of Exminster's stables that she might almost own them herself.

It was just a passing thought, but it made her feel again that strange repugnance which she could not explain.

She only knew that at the Ball tomorrow night she was quite certain he would be waiting not only to dance with her but to talk to her, and it was something she must avoid at all costs.

Because she and Penelope were so closely attuned to each other, her sister knew what she was thinking.

"Would it not be wonderful, dearest," she said, "if we both got engaged in the same night to a Duke? That would certainly startle the *Beau Monde*, and all those people who have refused to accept us would be falling over themselves."

"Are there such . . . people? I had no . . . idea."

"Oh, Alisa, your head is always in the clouds," Penelope complained. "You know quite well there are dozens of Balls to which we have not been invited, simply because we are either too pretty and put the hostess's plain daughters in the shade, or else because they do not consider us really grand enough to enter their exclusive, stuck-up circle."

Alisa merely looked surprised.

She had been so grateful to the hostesses who had invited them that she had never troubled to think there were others who deliberately refrained from doing so.

She could understand that Penelope, with her ambitions to be important, resented being left out, and if she did marry the Duke of Exminster there was no doubt that every door in London would be open to them both.

At the same time, when she thought of the red-faced Duke of Hawkeshead it seemed impossible to imagine him touching or kissing Penelope, but again she knew it was something she could not say.

"Nor do I want the . . . Duke of Exminster to . . . kiss me," she murmured beneath her breath.

* * *

The following day they took the pots to Mrs. Lulworth, who was delighted.

"I have a dozen ladies waiting for these to arrive," she said, "and I only hope they will be as good as the ones you made before."

"Of course they are!" Penelope answered.

"Well, you've fulfilled your obligation, Miss Penelope," Mrs. Lulworth said, "and now you will be delighted to hear that the two new evening-gowns are ready except for a few final touches."

Alisa looked at Penelope accusingly. She realised that her sister had not waited but had already ordered the gowns which she thought they both wanted.

"I should be angry with you, Penelope," she said when she thought Mrs. Lulworth was not listening.

"You ought to be grateful to me!" Penelope retorted. "You will have a new gown to wear tonight and another for the luncheon tomorrow which undoubtedly one of the Dukes will give for us."

It was impossible for Alisa to reply, because Mrs. Lulworth arrived back with two evening-gowns that were practically ready, and to Alisa's consternation two others that required a full fitting.

There were also two day-gowns for each of them. Although she wanted to protest, she felt it was hopeless and she just had to allow Penelope to have her own way.

There were bonnets to choose to wear with the day-gowns, and while they were being tried on she learnt the reason why Mrs. Lulworth was in such a good temper.

It transpired that quite a number of ladies had come to the shop because they had learnt that Mrs. Lulworth had made the gowns which she and Penelope wore.

The shop-keeper reeled off a list of her new patrons, and added:

"The Marchioness of Conyngham has asked me to attend her tomorrow morning. I'm very grateful to you both."

"We are so glad you are pleased," Penelope replied, "but I hope, Mrs. Lulworth, that your gratitude will show itself in the account you render us."

Alisa knew she would never have been able to say such a thing, but Mrs. Lulworth merely smiled and said:

"I thought you wouldn't have missed saying something like that, Miss Penelope, and I'll remember what I owe to you."

"Good!" Penelope exclaimed. "In which case I will have another bonnet, but in a different colour, to go with that last gown!"

When they arrived back in Islington Square there were more bouquets of flowers and more invitations.

Only as they were going upstairs to their bedrooms to start changing for the evening did Alisa say:

"Have you written to the Earl to thank him for taking us to the country yesterday?"

"I have not had time," Penelope prevaricated, "and anyway, I thought that you could write for both of us."

"I wrote and Henderson posted the letter for me," Alisa said, but as it was your idea in the first place, I think you ought to write too."

"I doubt if he will notice whether I do or I do not," Penelope replied, "and I expect anyway he would prefer a letter from *Madame* Vestris."

Alisa started.

"What have you . . . heard about *Madame* Vestris . . . and the . . . Earl?" she questioned.

"Somebody, I think it was Major Coombe, told me that she had said at some party or another that she judged her success in London by the fact that she had captured the British public and, what was far more difficult, the Earl of Keswick!"

Alisa did not reply.

She merely went into her bedroom and wondered why her new gown lying waiting for her on her bed looked so unattractive that she might just as well wear one of her old muslins.

Penelope had arranged that as the Duke was giving a party for them, he should also convey them to Hawkeshead House in Park Lane.

By the time they were dressed, a very impressive-looking carriage with the Duke's coat-of-arms emblazoned on the doors was waiting for them outside.

"You look lovely, dearest," Alisa exclaimed when she saw Penelope wearing her new gown.

Once again it was white, but there were magnolias round the hem and round the top of the bodice which revealed Penelope's white shoulders.

She wore a wreath of the same flowers on her golden hair, and Alisa knew that no tiara, however valuable, could have been more becoming.

Penelope looked like a water-maiden stepping out from a silver stream, and there was something very young, spring-like, and lovely about her which Alisa did not realise was echoed in herself.

Her gown was also white, but instead of the rather exotic magnolias it was decorated with small bunches of snow-drops, and they nestled in the softness of the tulle that encircled her shoulders like a white cloud.

If Penelope looked spring-like, Alisa was like Persephone, bringing light back to the world after a dark winter.

She was certainly not as sensational as her sister, and yet it would be hard for any man who saw her not to look again and not to find it difficult afterwards to see anybody else.

She only thought that Penelope looked beautiful, and she was content to follow behind her instead of leading the way as she should have done, being the elder.

"Be careful your wrap does not crush your gown," Penelope admonished her.

Then, having said good-night to their aunt, they hurried down the stairs to where the Duke's carriage was waiting.

Only as the horses moved off and they sat back against the comfortable, heavily padded seat did Alisa say hesitatingly:

"If the Duke does ... ask you tonight to ... marry him, dearest, please think ... seriously before you ... accept him."

"What is there to think about?" Penelope asked bluntly.

"Whether you will be ... happy with him. After all, he will be your husband and you will be ... together for the ... rest of your ... lives."

"Can you imagine always having a carriage like this to drive everywhere?" Penelope asked. "To be hostess of his house in Park Lane and his Castle in Kent? I believe too that he has half-a-dozen others in other parts of England."

"It is not . . . only what he . . . owns, but what he is."

"A Duke!" Penelope exclaimed irrepressibly.

It was hopeless, Alisa decided, to try to explain what she wanted to say.

She knew only that she wanted Penelope's happiness more than anything else in the world, but she could not help thinking it would be very difficult to be happy with the Duke of Hawkeshead.

Then she found herself thinking of the man Penelope called "her Duke" because she thought the same applied in her case.

What did it matter when they were alone together whether he was the Duke of Exminster or just plain "Mr."? They would be husband and wife, and he would also be the father of her children.

Quite suddenly Alisa knew that she could not marry the Duke, whatever Penelope might say.

She felt, because she was nervous of seeing him again, that she wanted to stop the coach and get out and run back to Islington. Or, better still, to return to the country so that the Duke would not know where she was and would be unable to find her.

Then she told herself that she was being very stupid.

Perhaps he would not propose to her. Perhaps like the Earl, he hand no intention of marrying anybody and was only being charming in sending her flowers because it was a fashionable thing to do.

But her intuition told her something else.

It was only a question of time before the Duke proposed, and unless she was to be faced with Penelope's reproaches and anger, she would have to accept him.

'I cannot do so . . . I cannot!' she thought despairingly.

She felt as if the comfortable carriage were taking her not to a Ball but to the guillotine.

Chapter Six

Looking round the Ball-Room at Hawkeshead House, Alisa thought it was the most attractive of all those in which they had danced.

In fact, the whole house was extremely impressive, and from the moment they had entered through the front door she had felt that Penelope was thinking what a perfect background it would be for her as a Duchess.

She thought the double staircase was in itself like a stage-set for a woman to look her best, as she ascended to where the Duke was receiving his guests with his mother beside him.

The Dowager's jewels, including a huge tiara that was almost like a crown on her head, seemed to be a glittering inducement to every girl who saw it. But Alisa thought they would also have to include the Duke in their consideration.

The way His Grace received Penelope was extremely revealing.

He was looking, Alisa thought, even more red-faced and unprepossessing than usual.

She tried to feel charitable towards him because he might become her brother-in-law, but she noticed that his cravat was already wilting, one of his decorations was crooked, and his silk stocking had a run in it.

'Perhaps he needs a wife to look after him,' she thought, and was glad that it would not be her task.

The Reception-Room was decorated with orchids and lilies, but the Ball-Room, obviously as a compliment to Penelope, was a bower of pink roses.

All along one side of the house there were long French windows that opened out onto a garden which as usual was lit by Chinese lanterns and fairy-lights.

Tonight they were all pink, and Alisa thought the Duke was certainly declaring his intenions to all the world.

She did not say anything to Penelope but she saw that there was a gleam of excitement in her sister's eyes, and when the Duke invited her to be his partner for the first dance, she knew that the Dowagers seated round the Ball-Room were already aware who would be the new Duchess.

Alisa noticed too that there were many different faces from those she had seen at the other parties they had attended.

She had an idea that the Duke and his mother moved in a society loyal to the old King and Queen which was more sedate that the fashionable *Beau Monde* who had circled round the Prince Regent when he lived at Carlton House.

Now, Alisa thought, they would certainly wish to be in favour with George IV and undoubtedly would be only too eager to grace the Coronation in July.

"What are you thinking about?" asked the Duke of Exminster, who was partnering her in the dance.

"The Coronation."

He laughed.

"Does anybody think of anything else at the moment?"

"You are not looking forward to it?"

"Most certainly not! As far as I am concerned it will be a long-drawn-out bore! It is only women, and of course the King, who enjoy all that dressing up and the endless ceremonial."

As the Duke spoke, his eyes were on Alisa's hair, and it suddenly struck her that he might be thinking that the Exminster strawberry-leaves would become her.

Quickly she looked away from him, and as she did so, she saw the King arriving, accompanied by the Marchioness of Conyngham and behind them several younger men, one of whom was the Earl of Keswick.

She felt her heart leap in an uncomfortable manner, but she could not help staring at him, realising that as usual he was looking bored and cynical.

The King, however, was greeting the Duchess of Hawkeshead effusively, and with the Duchess on his right and the Marchioness on his left he sat down on a sofa which stood on a raised dais, from where he could watch the dancing.

The gentlemen in attendance ranged themselves behind him, and because Alisa had no wish for the Earl to see her, she said quickly to the Duke:

"It is very hot, shall we go into the garden?"

"I think that is a very sensible suggestion," he replied.

They walked through one of the open windows, and the pink lanterns glowed against the dark branches of the trees while the stars overhead were just coming out.

It was certainly very romantic, but as she thought of it Alisa remembered that she had no wish to be alone with the Duke.

However, it was too late to retrace her steps, and she realised that he was leading her away from the lights of the house. As usual when a Ball was given where there was a garden, there were little alcoves and secluded seats where two people could talk intimately.

Alisa stopped.

"We must not go too . . . far," she said. "I have not seen Penelope for . . . some time."

"I am certain your sister can look after herself."

"As my aunt is not with us this evening," Alisa replied, "I have to chaperone Penelope, who is younger than I."

"I can think of a better way for you to do that," the Duke replied.

As he spoke he took Alisa by the arm and led her from the lighted path over the lawn to where there was a seat under an ash tree.

Alisa was just about to say that she would like to go back to the Ball-Room when the music stopped, and those who had been dancing came pouring out through the lighted windows into the garden.

There was nothing she could do but sit down on the seat the Duke had chosen, and she saw apprehensively that there were no other seats near them. They were in the shadow of the boughs and to all intents and purposes along.

Frantically she tried to think of how she could prevent him from saying what she was sure was in his mind, but while she was still trying to find the words, the Duke said:

"You are much too young, Alisa, to have to look after anybody, but if you wish to look after your sister more competently than you can do at the moment, I suggest the best way to do so would be to marry me!"

For a moment there was silence while Alisa tried to grasp the fact that she had received the proposal which she had been anticipating he might make, and which Penelope had been insistent she should accept.

Her head felt as if it were filled with cotton-wool, her throat seemed constricted, and she could do nothing but twist her fingers together.

"I know we have not known each other for very long," the Duke went on, "but from the first moment I sat beside you at dinner I knew you were not only beautiful but clever and everything I wanted in my wife. We will be very happy."

The way he spoke told Alisa that he had already assumed that she would accept his proposal. In fact, for him it was inconceivable that any woman would refuse him, let alone somebody of no social importance.

With an effort, and in a voice that did not sound like her own, Alisa said:

"I am deeply . . . honoured . . . Your Grace . . . that you should ask me to be your . . . wife . . . but as you say . . . we have known each other . . . only a very short . . . time."

"I have known you long enough to know that you will make me a very happy man," the Duke replied, "and as the King is here this evening, I would like him to be the very first to know of our engagement."

"Please . . . please," Alisa said frantically, "we are . . . not engaged . . . not yet . . . you must let me . . . think. I have been in London only a short while . . . and could not . . . consider . . . marriage with anybody . . . unless I knew them . . . well."

She did not look at the Duke, but she was aware that he was surprised at what she had said and his eyes were on her face.

"I am sure," he said after a moment, "that you would wish to be married before the Coronation. The Duchess of Exminster has a traditional role to play in such ceremonies, and I know that no Duchess could be more beautiful than you."

"Thank you . . . Your Grace," Alisa said in a very small voice. "I am . . . deeply sensible of the . . . honour it is for me to receive such a . . . proposal . . . but I . . . must think about it . . . I must be sure . . . that I will be able to . . . make you happy."

"I am quite sure of that," the Duke said complacently.

"Then could we both . . . think it . . . over for a few . . . weeks?"

"I have nothing to think about," he replied. "I want you, Alisa, and although I know you are young and perhaps it frightens you to think you will have to play such an important part in the Social World, I will look after you and you need not be afraid of making mistakes."

"You are . . . very kind," Alisa said breathlessly, "but I must . . . think about it . . . I must . . . be sure before I give you my answer."

There was a pause before the Duke replied, and Alisa knew he was surprised that she should prevaricate and not accept him immediately as he had expected.

"I am sure enough for both of us," he said at length.

He put out his hand to take hers.

"I promise you we will be very happy together, and tomorrow or the next day I will take you to meet some of my relatives."

The touch of his hand on hers gave Alisa again a feeling of repugnance that she had felt before.

Quickly she took her hand away and rose to her feet.

"I must go and . . . find Penelope . . . Your Grace," she said, and hurried away from him before he could follow her.

She sped across the lawn towards a different window from the one through which she had come with the Duke, and she found when she reached it that it did not lead into the Ball-Room but to a Sitting-Room at the side of it.

It was empty, but there was a door opening out of it into a room in which she could see card-tables and a number of gentlemen either playing or standing about with a glass in their hands.

She had discovered at the Balls they had already attended in London that there was always a room set aside where the older men who disliked dancing could gamble with one another and drink in comfort.

There was also a door which led to the passage, and as Alisa went towards it she heard a gentleman in the Card-Room say to another:

"Where's our host? I have not seen him for some time."

"Finding another bottle," a voice answered, "and I expect as usual he has lost count by now."

There was a burst of laughter at this, and just as Alisa was about to leave the Sitting-Room the gentleman who had spoken first said:

"I think he is more likely to be ravishing that attractive creature with whom he was dancing earlier in the evening!"

Alisa drew in her breath.

It was insulting that he should refer to Penelope in such a manner, and she thought, from the way he slightly slurred his words, that he also had been drinking.

Now she knew she must find Penelope and see if she was all right.

She did not know why, but when she had made Penelope an excuse for leaving the Duke, she had positively felt in some strange way she had often felt before that Penelope did need her.

Because they were so close, they often thought the same things and would laugh about it.

"We might be twins," Penelope had said more than once.

"I think really it is because we have always lived such a secluded life together in the countryside," Alisa had answered.

Now she was sure Penelope wanted her, and she walked down a corridor which contained some very fine pieces of furniture and a great number of valuable paintings.

Alisa had no idea where she was going, but she felt that if the Duke was proposing to Penelope, as was likely, he would not have taken her to the garden but to some quiet room whhere they could be alone.

There were a number of Sitting-Rooms on the ground

floor, all of which were discreetly lit and decorated with flowers.

As she peeped into them, some were empty but in others there were couples, obviously talking intimately, and in one she saw two people kissing passionately, which made her hurriedly move away.

She had almost reached the end of the passage which seemed to run the whole length of the house when she saw somebody in white come through a door and realised that she had found whom she was seeking. It was Penelope.

She hurried towards her, seeing as she did so that there was a large notice on the door marked: PRIVATE, and Penelope was shutting it behind her.

Then as she turned and saw Alisa standing only a few feet away, she gave a little cry.

At the same time, Alisa saw the expression on her face and exclaimed:

"What is the matter? What has happened?"

She could see that Penelope was trembling.

"What has upset you, dearest?" she asked, as her sister did not speak.

"I—I have killed—the Duke!"

For a moment Alisa felt that she must have misunderstood, but there was a stricken look in Penelope's eyes and her face was so pale that it was obvious something terrifying had occurred.

"What do you . . . mean, dearest?" she managed to ask.

"I have—killed him!" Penelope answered. "He is—dead—in that—room!"

As she spoke she stretched out her hands blindly, and Alisa put her arm round her.

She saw an open door beside them and through it another Sitting-Room with shaded lights and decorated with flowers, and it was empty.

She gently pulled Penelope into the room and closed the door behind them.

"What are you saying?" she asked. "Did you . . . really say . . . you had . . . killed the Duke?"

"After he asked me to marry him—he tried to—kiss me," Penelope answered, "and when I resisted him—he forced me down on a—sofa."

She made a sound that was almost like that of an animal in pain as she said:

"He was—horrible—beastly—and I—hated him!"

"Then what happened?" Alisa asked, as Penelope seemed unable to say any more.

"I—escaped from him, but when I tried to—get out of the room he—stopped me."

She paused before she could go on:

"It was—then that I realised he had had too much to—drink, and he was—behaving like an—animal!"

"Oh, dearest!"

"I picked up the—poker, and when he—rushed at me—again—I pushed it—hard into his—stomach."

She held her breath as if it was frightening to remember what she had done. Then before Alisa could speak she continued:

"He—doubled up for a moment—then I hit him and hit him—on top of the head. He fell down and I went on —hitting him!"

"Oh . . . how . . . could you!" Alisa breathed.

"I wanted to—hurt him. Then I—realised that he was—dead!"

Alisa put her arms round her to hold her, and Penelope asked:

"What—shall we do? I—cannot tell—anybody about it but—you."

Because Penelope sounded so helpless and so unlike herself, Alisa found a strength that she had never had before.

"Somebody must help us," she said. "You stay here, dearest, until I come back."

She felt as if Penelope hardly heard her, and she added:

"I will lock you in. Then you will not be disturbed by anybody. Do not be frightened. I will be back in a few minutes!"

"I am—frightened!" Penelope said. "Oh, Alisa, I am—very—frightened!"

"I will be as quick as I can."

Penelope did not reply. She merely put her hands over her face, and because she seemed suddenly small and pathetic, Alisa moved to the door with a determination that was very unlike herself.

She closed and locked the door, then holding the key in her hand she ran down the passage.

She knew there was one person who could help her now, and as she went in search of the Earl it flashed through her mind that they might have to hide somewhere or perhaps even leave England.

She thought that the Earl would be with the King in the Ball-Room, but as the music grew louder she passed a room in which there were a number of people drinking champagne, and there she saw him.

He was standing talking to Major Coombe, and, as there was no sign of the King, he was apparently for the moment free of his duties.

Without thinking of anything except that he was there and he must help them, Alisa went to his side.

The Earl was just saying something to the Major when, seeing Alisa at his elbow, he stopped in the middle of a sentence and looked at her in surprise.

"I must . . . speak to . . . you," Alisa said in a voice that was barely above a whisper but with a distinct tremor in it.

The Earl realised at once that something untoward had happened, for her eyes were stricken as Penelope's had been.

He put down the glass he was holding in his hand and moved a few steps towards an empty corner of the room.

"What is it?" he asked.

For a moment Alisa felt it was impossible to tell him, impossible for the words to come to her lips. Then, so quietly he could only just hear, she said:

"P-Penelope has . . . killed the . . . D-Duke!"

The Earl was still for a moment, and there was a question in his eyes, as if he thought he had either misunderstood what Alisa had said or she was playing some joke on him.

Then, as if he was convinced not so much by her words as by the look on her face, he said quietly:

"We will walk slowly from the room as if nothing unusual has happened."

Then in a voice that could be heard by many of the people standing near them he said:

"I am finding, Miss Wynton, that it is extremely hot in here, and I am not surprised that some people are feeling faint. Let us try to find somewhere cooler."

Then as she took a few steps beside him to cross the room to the door, the Earl said to Major Coombe, whom they had left standing alone:

"Why do you not come with us, James? I have something interesting to tell you."

The Major put down his glass.

"Then I shall certainly accompany you," he replied.

They walked at what seemed to Alisa a funereal pace, and only when they were outside the room and had moved away from several groups of people talking in the passage did the Earl ask:

"Where is Penelope?"

"I have . . . locked her in a . . . room where she . . . will not be . . . disturbed."

"That was very sensible of you," he replied.

They walked back the way Alisa had come, and now when they were free of the guests and there was nobody within earshot, Major Coombe asked:

"What is the matter? Where are we going?"

"I want your help, James," the Earl replied, and the Major said no more.

They reached the end of the long passage, and as Alisa saw the Earl's eyes on the room marked PRIVATE, she knew there was no need to explain to him where the Duke was lying.

As they stopped she felt that her hands were trembling so violently that she would be unable to open the door of the room where she had left Penelope, and without speaking she held the key out to the Earl.

He opened the door and as she walked inside he shut it behind her and she heard the key turn in the lock.

Penelope was sitting where she had left her. She was not crying, only staring blindly ahead of her in a manner of utter despondency and despair.

She went to the sofa and took Penelope's hand in hers.

"I have brought the Earl," she said, "and I am sure he will help us. Perhaps we can hide somewhere or go abroad, but whatever it may be, he is the only person who can arrange it."

"I was—wrong to—hit him so—hard." Penelope said, "but I was—frightened."

"I can understand that," Alisa said, "but you say he asked you to marry him?"

"He said—he was *going* to marry me," Penelope corrected. "Then he—grabbed me, and his lips hurt my cheek—and I knew he was—horrible and I—could not let him—touch me!"

Alisa put her arms round her sister to hold her close against her.

"He was—rough and beastly!" Penelope was saying.

"And I wanted to—get away—but he was big and—strong and I thought I—would not be able to—escape."

"You must not think about it," Alisa said. "It will not do any good."

"I am—sorry, Alisa, very sorry—I have spoilt—everything for you."

"There is no need to be sorry, not as far as I am concerned," Alisa answered. "I love you, Penelope, and it would not matter what you did, I should still go on loving you."

"Oh—Alisa—!"

Now the tears were in Penelope's eyes, and as she wiped them away Alisa thought she was suffering from shock and should have something to drink. But there was nothing in the room, and the only thing they could do was to sit and wait.

She could not think why the Earl was taking so long.

It would be impossible to conceal the Duke, and once he had confirmed that he was dead, he should be concerning himself with Penelope.

It was agonising to have to wait, not knowing what was happening, and Alisa in fact would have gone in search of the Earl if he had not locked her in.

Now Penelope was just staring in front of her, her hands hanging limply at her sides, and Alisa could think of nothing more to say.

She could only sit listening and waiting for the door to open and the Earl to join them.

Then suddenly there was the sound of the key turning in the lock, and he was there.

He walked through the door and for a moment she could not look at his face and felt afraid.

Then as she rose a little unsteadily to her feet, Penelope also rose to hers and gave a cry that seemed to echo round the silent room.

"Jimmy!" she exclaimed. "Oh, Jimmy!"

To Alisa's amazement, she ran towards Major Coombe, who had followed the Earl in through the door.

She flung herself against him and his arms went round her, holding her close against him.

"It is all right, my darling," he said. "He is not dead."

Penelope burst into tears, and as she did so Major Coombe bent his head and his lips were against her cheek.

Alisa stood staring at them in sheer astonishment until the Earl said quietly:

"What James has just said is true and the Duke is not dead, although Penelope has certainly been very rough with him!"

To her surprise there was just a hint of laughter in his voice, and as she looked up at him in a bewildered fashion, he said in an authoritative tone:

"Now, all of you listen to me."

Penelope raised her head from Major Coombe's shoulder.

"I—I thought I would be—hanged," she whispered.

"Nobody will hang you," he said. "I will make sure of that."

There were tears on Penelope's face, but now there was a light in her eyes and she looked, Alisa thought, very different from the stricken helpless girl who a few seconds before had been sitting beside her on the sofa.

"I love you!" Major Coombe said. "I will look after you and see that nothing like this ever happens again."

As he finished speaking he kissed her on the lips and Penelope put her arm round his neck and held him close to her.

Alisa was aware that the Earl was watching them with an undoubted twinkle in his eye. Then the Major said:

"We will talk about ourselves a little later, but now we have to listen to what Landon has planned."

Obediently Penelope looked towards the Earl, and Alisa in surprise realised that she was not in the least embarrassed that he had watched her being kissed.

Instead, she groped for her handkerchief, and when the Major handed her his, she gave him a beguiling smile before she wiped her cheeks.

"Now, attend to what I have to say," the Earl remarked. "James and I have made it appear that while the Duke was alone in his private Sitting-Room, a thief broke in through the window and assaulted him, robbing him of his watch, his jewellery, and any money he might have had on him. So now none of us can be implicated in any way in any crime."

He paused before he went on:

"You, Penelope, and James will go back to the Ball-Room to dance so that everybody can see you, and Alisa and I will go into the garden to dispose of the Duke's possessions in a flower-bed where they will ultimately be recovered."

"That is a very—clever plan!" Penelope exclaimed. "But are you—quite certain he is not—dead?"

"He will undoubtedly live to enjoy a great many more bottles of wine!" the Earl said drily. "Now come along, we cannot waste time here when we should be seen in a different part of the house."

"I do not know how to thank you," Penelope said.

She looked at Major Coombe and asked:

"Do I—look all right? Is my hair tidy?"

"You look lovely!" he answered.

There was a deep note in his voice which Alisa thought revealed his feelings very clearly.

"Walk slowly and look happy," the Earl commanded.

He opened the door as he spoke, and Penelope went out first. She was holding Major Coombe by the hand, and as they walked down the passage ahead of Alisa and the Earl they made no attempt to release each other.

It was impossible for Alisa to speak, because she

found that coming back from the depths of despair to find it was not as serious as she had feared had left her suspended, as it were, in mid-air.

She could only feel a surge of gratitude toward the Earl, and at the same time she felt as if she wanted to burst into tears and hide her face against his shoulder as Penelope had done with Major Coombe.

For a moment or two she could not adjust herself to the fact that Penelope had run to the Major as if she were a homing-pigeon returning to safety, that he had kissed her and that Penelope had put her arms round him to hold him close.

'So that is whom she loves!' Alisa thought, and found it impossible to understand why, loving James Coombe, she had been ready to accept the Duke.

However, she was not allowed to pursue her own thoughts, for the Earl was speaking to her so that as they mingled with the other people in the corridor it should appear that they were behaving in an entirely normal manner.

"I do not know whether Exminster told you earlier in the evening about his horse *Victorious*?" the Earl was saying.

"Y-yes . . . he did," Alisa managed to reply after a pause.

"*Victorious* is a very fine animal, but I would like to show you my *Apollo* who is his accredited rival," the Earl went on. "Whenever they run together they are always made equal favourites in the race, which is something that happens very rarely in the Racing World."

"No . . . I suppose it is . . . unusual!" Alisa forced herself to reply.

They reached the garden, and now as the Duke turned to walk towards the walls which were closest to the private Sitting-Room where the Duke lay injured, she knew what he was about to do.

She was not mistaken, for he took from his pocket a

handkerchief which he had tied in a knot and which contained what the imagined robber was supposed to have stolen from the Duke.

He glanced over his shoulder to see that there were no people near, then tossed it at the foot of an outside wall.

Then he deliberately trampled down some of the flowers that filled the bed in front of it, and as soon as he had done so, he took Alisa by the arm and walked her away to another part of the garden.

"That was . . . very clever of . . . you," was all she could manage to say when she could speak.

"It was the most sensible thing to do in the circum-stances."

"I am sure the . . . Duke should have . . . medical at-tention."

"You had better go back to the Ball-Room," the Earl replied. "I intend to deal with that now, and then I imagine you and Penelope will wish to go home."

"Yes, please . . . and as quickly as . . . possible," Alisa said, "I could . . . not dance any . . . more."

She spoke in a sudden panic, as if she was afraid she might have to dance with the Duke of Exminster again.

"Leave everything to me," the Earl said.

As they walked towards the Ball-Room they could see Penelope and Major Coombe standing just inside the door.

The music had stopped and the dancers once again were moving into the garden or going in search of the Supper-Room.

The Duke walked into the room and up to Penelope.

"Your sister has a headache," he said loudly enough to be overheard, "and I think it would be a good idea if you two had an early night."

"Yes, of course," Penelope agreed, and turned to Alisa to say:

"I am sorry, dearest. It must be the heat."

"Yes . . . of course. It has been very . . . hot," Alisa agreed.

"I am just going to explain to His Majesty that I am escorting you home," the Earl said.

Then as a servant passed him he said:

"Will you find His Grace? I think His Majesty will soon wish to leave."

"I will tell His Grace," the servant replied.

The Earl walked away in a different direction, and Major Coombe said:

"Let us go into the Hall and send a footman to get your wraps."

They waited in the Hall for only a few minutes before the Earl joined them.

"I found the Duchess with His Majesty," he said, "and I explained, Alisa, that you were not feeling well and I made excuses for both of you."

Alisa started as he spoke, realising that she had forgotten that the Duchess was acting as hostess for her son and they should have thanked her for the Ball.

"It is all right," the Earl said before she could speak. "I made out that you were worse than you are, being sure that otherwise people would think it strange that you should wish to leave the dance which had obviously been given in Penelope's honour."

There was an undoubted touch of sarcasm in the last words, but Alisa realised that Penelope was not listening but was only looking at James Coombe with starry eyes.

* * *

Driving back in the Earl's comfortable carriage, Alisa thought it very strange that she and the Earl sat in the back seat side by side while Penelope and James sat opposite them.

Quite unashamedly the Major put his arm round Penelope and she laid her head against his shoulder, as if she felt that was where she wanted to be and there was no need to pretend in front of her sister or the Earl.

They had driven some way from Hawkeshead House before Major Coombe said:

"If we are to honeymoon before the Coronation, when I shall be on duty, we will have to get married immediately!"

Alisa gasped, but Penelope answered:

"I can be ready tomorrow."

Major Coombe laughed.

"I shall need just a little longer than that, my darling. And I think it would be politic for you to meet my mother before we are actually married."

"Yes, of course," Penelope agreed, "but nothing seems to matter except that you love me."

"I will make you sure of that when we are married," James Coombe said, "and it will not be in more than three or four days' time."

Penelope gave a sigh of happiness and moved a little nearer to him, while Alisa felt as if the world had turned upside-down and she could hardly believe what wes happening.

As if to make sure she was not dreaming, she looked towards the Earl and saw that he was not looking at Penelope and James Coombe but at her.

It was impossible to see the expression on his face in the lights which occasionally flashed through the carriage-window, but even so, the mere fact that he was looking at her made Alisa feel shy.

Penelope was whispering something in James Coombe's ear, and as she did so he was holding her close against him with both his arms round her.

The fact that they had forgotten everybody except themselves made Alisa feel alone and a little lost.

She and Penelope had always been so close to each

other that now she could hardly believe that while she had spoken of him scornfully, Penelope had really loved James Coombe without even telling her.

There was no doubt that she was in love, and Alisa knew her too well not to be aware that there was a new note in her voice that had never been there before.

She could feel too a vibration coming from Penelope which was also r.ew, and which she knew was one of happiness and love.

'That is how I want to feel,' she thought, 'and I will never, never marry anybody unless I do feel that way.'

She decided that tomorrow she would write to the Duke of Exminster and thank him for his proposal and say once again that she was deeply honoured that he should wish her to be his wife, but she would make it quite clear that it was something that would never happen.

'I want to be in love,' she thought.

She felt that only when she could cry out as Penelope had done at the sight of James, and run towards him knowing that he was everything she wanted in the whole world, would she accept a man as her husband.

The horses were slowing down and she was aware that they were turning into Islington Square.

It was then, as if he knew what she was feeling, that the Earl reached out and Alisa felt his hand take hers.

The strength and warmth of his fingers were comforting, and as they tightened they aroused in her the same feeling that she had felt when he had kissed her.

She could feel the rapture of it moving through her body, as it had done then, and she knew as it rose from her breast into her throat, then to her lips, that she was in love, completely and hopelessly in love, with the Earl of Keswick.

Chapter Seven

Alisa awoke early after spending most of the night lying awake and thinking about the Earl.

She realised that her love was hopeless for if he had made up his mind that he would remain a bachelor, nothing and nobody would change it.

She could understand now why the women he had in his life were like *Madame* Vestris or occupied a position such as he had offered her.

At all the parties at which she had seen him, he had never seemed to be interested in any particular woman, and although the sophisticated beauties who were married clustered round him, he continued to look bored and cynical in the way to which she had grown accustomed.

"I love him!" she whispered to herself.

She knew that it would bring her no happiness to stay in London and go to parties and Balls when all she wanted was to be alone with him.

When she was called, she rose and dressed before she went to her sister's room, hoping that after all the dramatic happenings of the night before, Penelope would sleep late.

But she was awake, sitting up in bed and looking exquisitely lovely with her fair hair falling over her shoulders and her eyes shining.

139

"I have had a letter from Jimmy!" she cried before Alisa could speak.

"What does he say?"

"That he loves me, and that we will be married just as quickly as he can arrange it. Oh, Alisa, I am so happy!"

"I am glad, dearest, but I had no idea that you even liked Major Coombe!"

"I tried to hate him because I felt differently about him than about any other man I had ever met, and I was determined to be a Duchess!"

Penelope laughed, and it was a very attractive sound.

"How could I have been so stupid? How could a Duchess's coronet be as thrilling as Jimmy's kisses?"

Alisa could understand only too well, and she sat down on the edge of the bed to say:

"I am so very very happy for you, dearest! But please, we cannot afford a great many expensive gowns for your trousseau, because it would take me a long time to pay for them."

"What does it matter what I wear?" Penelope asked. "Jimmy thinks I look lovely in anything!"

Alisa stared at her sister, remembering what a fuss she had made about having new gowns. At the same time, she was apprehensive as to how much they still owed to Mrs. Lulworth.

She was just about to mention it when Penelope said:

"Jimmy has arranged for us to have luncheon with the Earl today, then he and I are going alone to buy my engagement-ring."

"I am sure you must be careful not to choose anything very expensive," Alisa said warningly.

Penelope nodded.

"I have already thought of that. I know Jimmy finds it difficult as it is, being in such an expensive Regiment, and that is why, like the Earl, he decided he would never get married."

Alisa smiled.

"He certainly seemed very eager to do so last night."

"He loves me," Penelope said in a rapt little voice.

Then as if she forced herself to think sensibly she said:

"We may have to live in a cottage, but I know that you will always help me, and when you are married to the Duke, at least I can wear the gowns for which you have no further use."

Alisa stiffened.

"Jimmy says that he is one of the richest Dukes and spends thousands a year on his horses, so he is not likely to be cheese-paring where you are concerned."

It was impossible for Alisa to reply, and Penelope went on:

"Perhaps, dearest, if you ask him very, very nicely he will give me my wedding-gown, I would like that to be beautiful for Jimmy's sake."

Alisa looked at her sister and said in a faltering voice:

"I . . . I have no . . . wish to marry the . . . Duke."

Penelope stared at her for a moment. Then she asked:

"Are you crazy? Of course you must marry him! He is not a drunken brute like the Duke of Hawkeshead, and although he is a lot older than you, everybody speaks of him warmly and says he is kind and considerate to his family and those he employs."

Alisa got down off the bed to walk across the room to stand at the window.

Penelope watched her go with a puzzled expression. Then she said:

"Please, dearest Alisa, be sensible about this. I know you have been much more idealistic about love than I have been until now, but there is not another Jimmy! There could not be, and you will make such a beautiful Duchess of Exminster."

"I do not want to talk about it," Alisa said, and walked out of the room, leaving Penelope alone.

* * *

Driving in the Earl's comfortable carriage which he had sent to fetch them to Keswick House for luncheon, Alisa was aware that Penelope was longing to return to the subject of her marriage to the Duke of Exminster.

She knew her sister so well that she was aware that she was feeling a little embarrassed but at the same time was determined that Alisa's future should be settled as well as her own.

She began to speak of how fond Jimmy was of riding and how hard it was for him not to be able to afford fine horse-flesh of his own.

"The Earl is very kind to him and lends him his hunters and even his Phaeton," Penelope said, "but it would be far easier for him to borrow from a brother-in-law."

Alisa did not protest, and Penelope went on to speak of the many advantages there would be for both her and Jimmy if Alisa was married to the Duke.

Because Alisa had always allowed Penelope to take the lead in anything they did, she felt as if her will was being sapped away and she would not have the strength to go on fighting.

She had already written the letter she had planned to the Duke, and now she had it in her reticule, intending to post it after she had made it clear to Penelope that she would not accept him as her husband.

"The one thing I have always longed to do," Penelope was saying, "is to wear a tiara, and as the Exminster jewels are famous, I know, dearest, that you will sometimes let me borrow one of yours."

Alisa took a deep breath.

"Penelope," she said, "I cannot . . . I will . . . not . . ."

As she spoke the words, the carriage came to a

standstill and she realised that they were outside the
Earl's house in Berkeley Square.

"We are here!" Penelope cried excitedly. "And I am
sure Jimmy will have come off parade by now."

The carriage-door was opened and she jumped out
before Alisa and hurried up the steps as if she could not
wait another moment before she saw the man she
loved.

James Coombe was with the Earl in the Library, and
as soon as the two sisters were announced, Penelope ran
towards him with a little cry.

"Thank you for my lovely letter which I found when I
woke up this morning!" she said. "I have read and read
it until I know it by heart."

James Coombe smiled at her and raised her hand to
his lips.

Alisa thought that Penelope in ignoring their host
was being rude, and hastily she curtseyed to the Earl.

"Good-morning, Alisa!" he said. "I hope you slept
well."

"Yes . . . thank . . . you."

She tried to speak calmly, but she felt as if he must
be aware that her heart was beating violently in her
breast, and it was difficult to look at him.

"I have good news for you."

"What is it?"

"I was informed this morning by several of my callers
that our host last night had been savagely assaulted by a
thief who entered his private Sitting-Room and, having
knocked him unconscious, robbed him!"

Alisa clasped her hands together and found it difficult
to breathe.

"Then an hour ago," the Earl went on, "I sent a
servant to enquire as to how His Grace was faring, and
I was informed that the doctors are satisfied with his
condition, which is not dangerous, although he is heavily
bruised."

Alisa gave a deep sigh of relief, Then she asked in a low voice:

"You do not . . . think that he will . . . tell anybody who . . . hit him?"

It was difficult to ask the question, and the Earl smiled before he replied:

"I think no man would admit to being knocked unconscious by a woman, especially one who is so delicately made and beautiful as your sister."

"You are . . . sure about . . . that?"

"Quite sure, so stop worrying!"

It was an order, and Alisa said meekly:

"I will . . . try."

Jimmy told Penelope the same news, and when they went in to luncheon, Alisa thought everybody seemed to be in extraordinarily good spirits.

There was champagne to celebrate Penelope and James's engagement, and as the meal finished the Earl lifted his glass and toasted them.

"To your happiness!" he said. "And may your future be as golden as it seems now!"

"That is a lovely toast!" Penelope cried. "And you know that everything that has happened to us is all thanks to you."

The Earl raised his eye-brows, and she said:

"I have told Jimmy that it was your fifty pounds that made us able to buy beautiful gowns in which we could call on the Marchioness of Conyngham."

As she spoke, Alisa made a little sound because she was upset, and Penelope said quickly:

"I am sorry, dearest, I should have asked you first if I might tell Jimmy, but I cannot have any secrets from him, Forgive me."

"It is all . . . right," Alisa answered.

It was impossible, however, for her to look at James Coombe, thinking that Penelope must have explained why the Earl had given her such a large sum of money, which was something she had hoped nobody would ever know.

As if to save her from being embarrassed, the Earl said:

"As I understand that Penelope said at the time it was a gift from the gods, and so we must therefore thank them, because in some obscure way of their own, which undoubtedly the Duke has found extremely regrettable, it has brought you two together."

"Of course, a gift from the gods!" Penelope exclaimed, "and the gift I have received is Jimmy."

"I shall always be extremely grateful," James Coombe said, "and we must, my darling, make a proper thank-offering, whatever that may be."

"I can think of quite a number I would accept," Penelope said, looking at him from under her eye-lashes, and for the moment they both forgot there was anybody else in the room with them.

The Earl pushed back his chair.

"If you two are going shopping," he said, "I will order my carriage for you, and I suggest you leave immediately, before Bond Street becomes too crowded and your secret will be out before your relations have time to assimilate the good new."

"Yes, of course," James agreed, rising to his feet. "Come along, my beautiful, I intend to chain you to me with a ring that symbolises that you will be mine for eternity!"

"That will not be long enough for me!" Penelope answered.

She linked her arm through Alisa's and they walked from the Dining-Room together.

"Did you hear from the Duke this morning?" she asked as they walked down the corridor.

"Some flowers . . . arrived just before we . . . left," Alisa replied hesitatingly.

"Good! That gives you an excuse to write to thank

him and tell him about Jimmy and me. There is nothing more infectious than the engagement of somebody one knows, and I am quite certain he will call this evening and propose to you."

Alisa did not reply.

She knew that if she told Penelope that the Duke had already proposed and she had actually written a letter refusing him, there would be a scene.

They went to the Library, where Penelope had left her bonnet which she had taken off before luncheon.

She put it on in front of the mirror and James tied the ribbons under her chin.

As he did so, she looked so lovely that, as if he could not help himself, he kissed her on the lips. Then he said to the Earl:

"We will not be long. Look after Alisa until we come back!"

"Yes, do that," Penelope said. "And try to persuade her to be sensible, for at the moment she is being very foolish!"

"In what way?" the Earl enquired.

Penelope smiled.

"She has to make up for my short-comings where our plan is concerned."

She did not say any more but left the room with James, and the door shut behind them.

Now that she was alone with the Earl, Alisa felt shy, and at the same time, because he was near her and because he looked so handsome, she felt her heart begin to beat frantically.

She could not help remembering that it was in this room that he had kissed her.

It was in this room that she had realised that a kiss could give her a rapture that made her feel as if her feet no longer touched the ground and her head was among the stars.

Because she was frightened that he would guess what

she was thinking, she walked to one of the book-cases to look at the books as she had done the first time she had come to his house.

"I presume the plan to which your sister was referring," he said behind her, "is that you should be, as she put it, 'the Gunning Sisters, up-to-date.'"

"That. . . . was what . . . Penelope meant us to . . . do," Alisa agreed, "but she has fallen in . . . love."

There was silence. Then the Earl said:

"Are you telling me that neither of you are aware that Penelope is in fact following very closely in the footsteps of Elizabeth Gunning?"

Alisa turned round.

"She would have done so if, as she had intended, she had married the Duke," she replied. "But, having fallen in love with an ordinary soldier, she realises that he can give her much . . . more than a coronet."

There was a faint smile on the Earl's lips as he said:

"James has been more astute than I gave him credit for. He has always hoped to be loved for himself, and that is what he has achieved."

"Of course," Alisa said, "and although they may be very poor, they have the only thing that . . . really . . . matters."

There was a little tremor in her voice as she said the last words. Then, looking puzzled, she said:

"I do not understand what you mean when you say that Penelope has followed in the footsteps of Elizabeth Gunning."

"That is something your sister will undoubtedly learn when she meets James's mother, but I will tell you what you obviously do not know," the Earl said, "which is that James is heir-presumptive to the Duke of Roehampton!"

Alisa stared at him as if she could not believe what she had heard. Then she asked:

"If that is true, why did James not tell Penelope?"

"The truth of the matter is that I do not think he is particularly interested in his prospects," the Earl said. "The present Duke is very old and in ill health. He is unmarried, and his brothers produced only daughters, with the result that James's father, who was a distant cousin, had he lived would have come into the title. But now it will be James's in the not-too-far-distant future."

Alisa clasped her hands together and gave a little cry of delight.

"That will be wonderful for Penelope, and now . . . I need not . . ."

She stopped, realising that what she had been about to say in her excitement was something about which she should remain silent.

"I should be interested to hear the end of that sentence," the Earl said.

Alisa turned round again to the book-case and her back was towards him.

"It was . . . not important."

"I think it was!"

She shook her head, then realised that he had come nearer to her before he said:

"Turn round, Alisa! I want to know what you were about to say."

"It is . . . nothing to do with . . . you."

Then she gave a little gasp as she felt the Earl's hands on her shoulders, turning her round.

He looked down at her and she was aware that his eyes were looking at her in that penetrating manner which always made her feel shy.

At the same time, because he was touching her, she felt a thrill go through her, and she thought wildly that if he would kiss her once again, it would be the most wonderful thing that could possibly happen.

"I want you to answer me truthfully." the Earl said. "Are you intending to accept Exminster?

Because he sounded grim and his fingers tightened painfully on her shoulders, Alisa felt herself tremble.

"Penelope . . . told me I . . . had to . . . so that I could . . . help her."

"So you have said 'yes'!"

"No . . . no!" Alisa cried. "I . . . cannot . . . marry him, and I have . . . written to . . . tell him so."

The Earl's fingers relaxed and she was free.

"And when Penelope marries," he asked, "what do you intend to do with yourself?"

"I will . . . go home and be with . . . Papa."

"And that will make you happy? After all, Exminster is not the only man in the world, although I doubt if you will get a better offer."

"I could not . . . marry anybody unless I . . . loved him in the . . . same way that . . . Penelope loves Jimmy."

"And you think it might be impossible for you to find such a man?"

Alisa drew in her breath.

She wondered what the Earl would say if she told him she had found somebody she loved overwhelmingly, completely, with all her heart and with all her mind, and that it was impossible for any other man to mean the same.

"I . . . shall be . . . all right."

"That is not what I asked you."

She could not answer him, and after a moment he said:

"What has made you decide that you will not marry Exminster?"

That was an easy question to answer, Alisa thought, and she replied:

"I do not . . . love him!"

"How do you know that?"

She glanced up at him in surprise because the question seemed rather foolish.

Then, because he was looking at her in a strange way, she felt the blood rising in her cheeks.

"When I kissed you the first time you came here," the Earl said, "I realised you were very inexperienced and very innocent, I was quite sure you knew nothing about men and less about love."

"That . . . was . . . true," Alisa murmured.

"And yet now you know you do not love one of the most eligible men in the *Beau Monde*. How do you know that?"

Alisa made a helpless little gesture with her hand.

"Answer me!" the Earl insisted.

"It is . . . difficult to explain," she faltered, "but I do not . . . want him to touch me . . . and I know that if he . . . did, I would not . . . feel like I . . . did . . ."

She stopped, aware that what she was going to say would be very revealing.

" . . . like you did when I kissed you," the Earl finished, and his arms went round her.

She made a little sound, but she did not struggle, and he said:

"Shall we find out if the second time we kiss each other is as wonderful as the first?"

He did not wait for her answer, but his lips were on hers and Alisa knew at the first touch of them that this was what she had been longing and yearning for and thought she would never know again.

The strength of his arms holding her against him and the wonder of his kiss brought the rapturous feeling that she had known before, moving through her breasts, up her throat, and onto her lips.

Then he was carrying her into the sky and they were one with the stars.

She felt thrill after thrill rippling through her until her whole body quivered with an ecstasy that was so intense that it was almost a physical pain.

He drew her closer and still closer until the feelings he was arousing in her were so glorious, so incredibly marvellous, that Alisa felt she must have died and reached Heaven.

Then he raised his head and said in a voice that sounded strange and a little hoarse:

"Is that the sort of love you want?"

Because she was bewildered, bemused, and radiantly happy, Alisa could no longer think but only stammer:

"I . . . love you . . . and I . . . could not . . . marry anybody . . . unless they could . . . make me feel . . . like this."

Then the Earl's mouth held hers captive again, and she wished she could remain in the Heaven to which he had taken her, and never return to earth.

A short time, or a long time, later—it was impossible to judge—the Earl looked down into her shining eyes and at her lips red and soft from his kisses.

"You are so ridiculously beautiful," he said unsteadily, "and somebody has to look after you."

It flashed through Alisa's mind that he was going to make the same proposition to her that he had made the first time he had kissed her, and she stiffened.

Knowing what she was thinking, he laughed gently before he said:

"You are aware that Maria Gunning married an Earl, and we must follow her story exactly."

"M-marry?"

It was hard to say the word, and she was not certain whether she said the word aloud or her lips only mouthed it.

"Must I ask you properly?" the Earl enquired. "Will you, my lovely little Alisa, marry me? It is the least you can do, after haunting me until it is impossible for me to exorcise you from my thoughts. You are always in my mind, my heart, and my eyes."

"Did you . . . try to . . . forget me?" Alisa whispered.

"You disappeared and I thought I would never find you again."

"But you . . . tried?"

"I sent half-a-dozen women to ask Mrs. Lulworth for the creams you had sold to *Madame* Vestris."

"She did not . . . know who . . . I was."

"Nor did I."

"And you . . . really minded?"

"I wanted you and I intended to have you!" the Earl said. "If you feel you cannot marry a Duke, I assure you that ever since we met I have been unable to see, hear, or realise that there is any other woman in the world."

His lips twisted for a moment in the mocking way she knew so well as he asked:

"What have you done to me, my darling? I would have bet my entire fortune that no woman would be able to make me feel as I do now."

"You . . . really . . . love me?"

"I adore you! I cannot live without you! Is that what you want me to say?"

"I cannot . . . believe it! I have . . . loved you ever since you first . . . kissed me, but I never . . . thought you would . . . love me."

The Earl did not answer. He merely kissed her again.

When finally he set her free, Alisa's cheeks were flushed and she felt as if her whole being had come alive, yet she was no longer herself but a part of him.

"How can . . . everything be so . . . wonderful?" she cried. "Penelope has found . . . somebody to love, and you . . . love me!"

"I am sure we can explain it as a gift from the gods," the Earl said, "but it is a gift that I shall treasure, protect, love, and be extremely jealous of for the rest of my life."

As he spoke he drew her almost roughly back into his arms and said:

"How dare you ever consider marrying the Duke? You are mine as you were meant to be since the beginning of time. If I had had any sense I would have kept you prisoner the first day you came into this room and never let you go!"

The masterfulness about the note in his voice and the way he was holding her made Alisa feel thrills like shafts of sunlight running through her.

The Earl was exactly as she had always dreamt a real man would be: authoritative, commanding, and yet at the same time kind and understanding, and when necessary a haven of security.

"You are so . . . wonderful!" she cried. "How can I have been so . . . lucky as to . . . find you?"

"In a very unlikely place," he replied a little drily.

She knew he was thinking of *Madame* Vestris's dressing-room, and she said:

"If it had not been for three pots of face-cream, I would never have gone . . . there, and I would never have found . . . you. How . . . extraordinary that such little things should lead to anything so . . . utterly and completely marvellous."

"I am deeply grateful to those three pots," the Earl answered, "but selling them and visiting actresses is something you will never do again."

"It is . . . all like a . . . fairy-story."

"Which one day we will tell our children."

He watched for the colour that flooded into Alisa's cheeks. Then he smiled and with a note of unmistakable triumph in his voice said:

"A gift from the gods, and that, my precious one, is the love which we shall never lose and is ours today, tomorrow, and for the rest of eternity."

Then he was kissing her, fiercely, passionately, possessively, until Alisa knew they were no longer human but one with the gods themselves.

ABOUT THE AUTHOR

BARBARA CARTLAND, the world's most famous romantic novelist, who is also an historian, playwright, lecturer, political speaker and television personality, has now written over 300 books.

She has also had many historical works published and has written four autobiographies as well as the biographies of her mother and that of her brother Ronald Cartland, who was the first Member of Parliament to be killed in W.W. II. This book has a preface by Sir Winston Churchill and has just been republished with an introduction by Sir Arthur Bryant.

Barbara Cartland has sold 200 million books over the world, more than half of these in the U.S.A. She broke the world record in 1975 by writing twenty-three books and the four subsequent years with 20, 21, 23 and 24. In addition her album of love songs has just been published, sung with the Royal Philharmonic Orchestra.

Barbara Cartland, who is a Dame of the Order of St. John of Jerusalem has championed the cause for old people and founded the first Romany Gypsy Camp in the world.

Barbara Cartland is deeply interested in Vitamin Therapy and is President of the British National Association for Health. Her book the *Magic of Honey* has sold in millions all over the world.

She has a magazine *The World of Romance* and her Barbara Cartland Romantic World Tours will, in conjunction with British Airways, carry travelers to England, Egypt, India, France, Germany and Turkey.